The Innocent Adultery
& Other Short Novels

Paul Scarron

BENJAMIN BLOM · New York/London · 1968

First published 1892
Reissued 1968 by
Benjamin Blom, Inc. Bronx, N.Y. 10452
and 56 Doughty Street, London WC 1, England

Library of Congress Catalog Card Number 67-29562

Printed in the United States of America

Translated by Tom Brown, et. al., 1700

SCARRON'S NOVELS.

ÆTATIS SVÆ 31.°

SCARRON

From the frontispiece to his works engraved by Della Bella

NOVEL I.

AVARICE CHASTISED;

OR,

THE MISER PUNISHED.

IT is not quite a thousand years ago since a pretty younker, who was full as ambitious as poor, and had a greater itch to be thought a gentleman than a rational creature, left the mountains of Navarre, and came in company with his father to find that at Madrid which was not to be got in his own country, I mean wealth and riches ; which are sooner acquired at court than any other place, and indeed are seldom obtained there but by importunity and impertinence. He had the credit, I cannot inform you how it came about, to be received as a page by a certain prince, which quality in Spain is not so gainful as that of a lackey in France, and not much more honourable. When he first put on his livery, he was about twelve years old, and from that very moment might be termed the thriftiest page in the world. All his worldly stock, not to reckon his expectations, that were very big, consisted of a wretched bed set up in a garret, which he had hired in that quarter of the town where his master lived, and where he pigged every night with his venerable father, who may be said to have been rich in grey hairs, because by procuring him the charity of well-disposed persons, they helped to maintain

him. At last the old gentleman trooped off, at which his
unrighteous son rejoiced, fancying himself already enriched
by that which his father did not spend. From that very
hour he enjoined himself so severe and strict an abstin-
ence, and practised so wonderful a frugality, that he spent
not a farthing of that little money his master gave him to
keep body and soul together. It is true he did this
at the expense both of his belly, which often grumbled at
him for it, and of all his acquaintance. Don Marcos (for
that was our hero's name) was of a stature a little below
the common pitch ; and for want of due repairing the
decays of his pigmy carcass, became in a short time as
slender as a lath, and as dry as a deal-board. When he
waited on his master at table, he never took away a plate
with any meat in it but he dexterously whipped the better
part into his pocket ; and because it could not so well con-
tain soups and such-like liquids, he made money of a great
number of torches' ends, which he had scraped together
with much industry, and thereby bought him a pair of tin
pockets ; by the help of which he soon began to perform
miracles for the advancement of his fortune.

Misers are for the most part careful and vigilant, and
these two good qualities, joined to the furious passion
which Don Marcos had to become rich, made his master to
take such a fancy to him, that he was resolved never to
part with so excellent a page. For this reason he made
him wear a livery till he was thirty years old. But at last
this phœnix of a servant, being obliged to undergo the
tonsor's hands too often to clear him of his ungodly beard,
his master metamorphosed his page into a gentleman, and
thus made him what heaven never designed him to be. Now
you must know his revenues were hereby augmented by
the addition of several reals a day ; but instead of increasing likewise his expenses, our spark shut his purse so much
the closer, as his new employ, one would have thought, might
have obliged him to open it. He had heard stories of some

of his profession, who for want of a valet would call up
your fellows that cry brandy about streets in a morning, to
make their beds and sweep their chambers, under pretence
of buying some of their liquor ; and of others, who in the
winter got themselves undressed at night by your criers of
grey peas, or link-boys. But as this was not to be done
without some sort of injustice, and in regard our Don
Marcos made a conscience of wronging every one but himself, he thought it much better to shift as well as he could
without a valet. He never burnt but an inch of candle in
his chamber but what he stole ; and to manage it with more
economy always began to unbutton himself in the street at
the very place where he lighted it, put it out as soon as he
got to his lodgings, and so tumbled in to bed in the dark.

But still finding there was a cheaper way of going to bed,
his busy inventing genius set him upon making a hole in
the wall which divided his room from that of his neighbour, who no sooner lighted his candle but our Don
immediately opened his hole, and by that means received
light enough to do anything he had occasion for. Being
not able to dispense with himself from wearing a tilter at
his breech, by reason of his noble descent, which required
it of him, he clapped a lath into a scabbard, wore it one
day on the right, and the next on the left side, in order to
use his breeches to some sort of symmetry, and because his
trusty whinyard would wear them out the less, being
equally divided between the right and the left. At break
of day he stood at the street-door, begging in God's name
for a cup of water of every tankard-bearer that passed by,
and thus furnished himself with enough of that element to
serve him several days. He would often come into the
common hall, where his master's other servants used to
take their repasts, and whatever he saw them eat was
sure to commend it to the skies, to give him some sort of
privilege to taste it. He never laid out a farthing in wine,
yet drank more or less every day, either by sipping of that

which was publicly cried about streets, or else by stopping porters that were carrying some to the taverns, whom he would ask to give him a taste of their wine, that if he liked it he might know where to send for it. Once riding towards Madrid upon a mule, he so dexterously cheated the eyes of his inn-keepers, that he fed trusty Dapple with the straw of the beds where he lay ; but the very first day of his journey, being weary of paying for his servant's dinner, who was the first he ever had, he pretended he could not drink his landlord's wine, and therefore sent the poor fellow to find out better, a full league at least from the inn where he then was. The servant accordingly beat the hoof thither, relying upon his master's honour, who nevertheless fairly gave him the slip, and so the wretch was forced to beg all the way to Madrid. In short, Don Marcos was the living picture of avarice and filching, and was so well known to be the most covetous devil in Spain that at Madrid he advanced himself into a proverb, for they there called a pinching miser a Don Marcos. His master and all his friends told a thousand merry stories of him, and that even before his face, because he understood raillery to perfection, and would stand a jest as well as a managed horse will fire. It was a usual saying with him, that no woman could be handsome if she loved to take nor ugly if she gave money, and that a wise man ought, never to go to bed, unless for the satisfaction of his conscience he had turned the penny the same day.

His excellent theory, seconded by a most exact practice, had brought him together by that time he was forty years old, above 10,000 crowns in silver, a prodigious sum for a grandee's gentleman to get, especially in Spain. But what may not a man save in the compass of many years who steals all he can both from himself and other people? Don Marcos having the reputation of being rich, without being either a debauchee or a gamester, was soon courted in marriage by abundance of women, who loved the money more than the man, and whose number in all parts of the world is great. Among others that offered to carry the marriage yoke with him, he met a woman whose name was Isidore, who passed for a widow, though in truth she had never been married, and appeared much younger than she was, by patching, painting, and tricking up herself, in all which mysteries she was skilled to admiration. The world judged of her wealth by her way of living, which was expensive enough for one of her condition ; and those who frequently guess at random, and love to magnify matters, bestowed on her at least three thousand livres a year and some ten thousand crowns in plate, jewels, and the like convenient moveables. The fellow that proposed her to Don Marcos for a wife, was a notable sharper, one that trucked in all sorts of merchandise, but his principal sub- sistence was selling of maidenheads, and making of matches. He spoke to Don Marcos of Isidore in such advantageous terms that he set him upon the tenter-hooks to see this miracle (a curiosity he had never expressed for any woman before), and so effectually persuaded our un- thinking cully that she was rich, and the widow of a certain cavalier, descended from one of the best families in Andalusia, that from that very instant he had an itch to be married to her. The same day this proposal was made to him, our marriage-pimp, whose name was Gamara, came to call upon him, to introduce him into Isidore's com- pany. Our covetous hunks was ravished to see the neat- ness and magnificence of the house into which Gamara conducted him, but he was much more so when this master of the ceremonies assured him it belonged to Isidore. He was perfectly transported at the richness of the furniture, the alcoves, and rooms of state, and a pro- fusion of sweet scents, that rather seemed proper for a lady of the highest quality than one that was to be a wife to a grandee's gentleman and no better. Then as for the mistress of this enchanted castle, he took her for a goddess. Don Marcos found her busy at work between a damsel and a chamber-maid, both so beautiful and charming, that whatever aversion he had to expensive living, and a great number of servants, yet he resolved to marry Isidore, were it only for the vanity to be master of two such charming creatures. Whatever Isidore said to him was uttered so discreetly that it not only pleased but perfectly ravished him ; and what contributed to make an entire conquest of his heart, was a collation as nice as neatly served up, where the clean linen and the silver plate were all of a piece with the other rich movables.

There sat down to this entertainment a young gentleman very well dressed and well made, whom Isidore pretended to be her nephew. His name was Augustine, but his good aunt called him Augustinet, although the pretty baby was above twenty years old. Isidore and Augustinet strove who should make Don Marcos most welcome, and during the repast helped him to all the choicest bits. Now whilst our trusty miser laid about him like a harpy, and crammed his half-starved guts with victuals enough to have lasted him eight days, his ears were charmed by the melodious voice of the damsel Marcella, who sung two or three passionate airs to her harpsichord. Don Marcos lost no time, but fell on like a devil, it being at another's expense. The collation ended with the day, whose light was supplied by that of four large candles in silver sconces, of admirable workmanship and weight, which Don Marcos at that moment designed within himself to reform into one single lamp, so soon as he was married to Isidore. Augustinet took a guitar and played several sarabands and other tunes, to which that cunning jilt Marcella, and Inez the chamber-maid danced admirably well, striking their castanets exactly to the time of the guitar. The discreet Gamara whispered Don Marcos in the ear, that Isidore never sat up late ; which hint our civil gentleman taking immediately, rose from his seat, made her a thousand compliments and

protestations of love, more than he had ever done to
any female, wished her and the little Augustinet a good
night, and so left them at liberty to talk of him what they
thought fit.

Don Marcos, who was up to the ears in love with Isidore,
but much more with her money, protested to Gamara, who
accompanied him to his lodgings, that the charming widow
had entirely gained his affections, and that he would give
one of his fingers, with all his soul, that he were already
married to her, because he never saw a woman more made
to his mind ; although in sober truth he confessed, that
after marriage he would retrench somewhat of that endless
ostentation and luxury of hers.

" She lives more like a princess than the wife of a private
man," cries the prudent Don Marcos to the dissembling
Gamara ; " and she does not consider," continued he, " that
the movables she has, being turned into money, and this
money being joined to mine, we may be able between us to
purchase a pretty handsome estate, which by God's blessing
and my own industry, may make a considerable fortune for the
children Providence shall bestow on us. And if our marriage," proceeded he, " should prove without issue, then since
Isidore has a nephew, we will leave him all, provided I like
his behaviour, and find him no way addicted to ill hus-
bandry." Don Marcos entertained Gamara with these
discourses, or somewhat of the like nature, till he came
before his own door. Gamara took leave of him after he had
given him his word that next morning he should conclude
his marriage with Isidore, by reason, he said, affairs of this
nature were soon broke off by delays, as by the death of
either of the parties. Don Marcos embraced his worthy
marriage-jobber, who immediately after went to give Isidore
an account in what disposition of mind he had left her lover.
In the meantime our amorous coxcomb takes an end of a
candle out of his pocket, fixes it to the point of his sword,
and having lighted it at a lamp, which burnt before a

public crucifix hard by, not without dropping a few hearty ejaculations for good success in his affair, opened the door of the house where he lodged, and repaired to his wretched bed, but that rather to think of his amour than to sleep.

Gamara came to visit him next morning, and brought him the agreeable news that his business was done with Isidore, who wholly left it to his discretion to appoint the day of marriage. Our besotted lover told Gamara he was upon thorns till it was over, and that if he were to be married that very day, it would not be so soon as he wished. Gamara replied, it lay solely in his own power to conclude it whenever he pleased ; when Don Marcos embracing him, conjured him to use all his diligence to get the contract dispatched that very day. He appointed Gamara to give him a meeting after dinner, while he went to his master's levee, and waited on him at table. Both met exactly at the time of assignation, and then immediately went to Isidore's house, who received them much better than the day before. Marcella sang, Inez danced, Augustinet played upon the guitar, and Isidore, the principal actress of this farce, gave her spouse that was to be a noble repast, for which she knew well enough how to make herself full amends afterwards. Gamara brought a notary, who perhaps was a counterfeit one. The articles of marriage were signed and sealed. It was proposed to Don Marcos to play a game at *primera* to pass away the time. "Heaven bless me !" cried the astonished Don Marcos, "I serve a master who would not let me live a quarter of an hour with him, if he knew I was a gamester ; but, God be praised, I don't so much as know the cards."

"How much does it delight me," replies Isidore, "to hear Signor Don Marcos talk after this manner. I daily preach the same doctrine to my nephew Angustinet here, but your young fellows are not a farthing the better for all the good advice that is given them. Go, foolish, obstinate boy," says she to Augustinet, "go and bid Marcella and

Inez make an end of their dinner, and come and divert us with their castanets."

While Augustinet went to call up the maids, Don Marcos, stroking his whiskers with admirable gravity, thus carried on the discourse ; " If Augustinet," says he, " has a mind to keep in my favour, he must renounce gaming and staying out late at nights. If he'll keep good hours, I am content with all my heart he should lie in my house ; but I'll have my windows barred, and doors locked and bolted before I go to bed : not that I am in the least jealous in my temper, for I think nothing can be more impertinent, especially where a man has a virtuous wife, as I am going to have ; but houses, where there is anything to lose, cannot be too well secured against thieves ; and for my part I should run distracted if a villain of a thief, without any other trouble than that of carrying off what he found, should rob me in an instant of what my great industry had been scraping together for many years ; and therefore," continues Don Marcos " I forbid him gaming and rambling at nights, or the Devil shall roast him alive, and I will renounce the name of Don Marcos."

The choleric gentleman uttered these last words with so much vehemence and passion, that it cost Isidore abundance of fair speeches to put him in a good humour again. She conjured him not to trouble himself about the matter, assuring him that Augustinet would not fail to answer his expectation in all points, because he was the most tractable and the best-conditioned boy that ever was known. The coming in of Augustinet and the dancers put a stop to this discourse, so they spent the greatest part of the night in dancing and singing.

Don Marcos being loath to give himself the trouble to walk to his lodgings so late, would by all means have persuaded Isidore to give her consent that they might live together from that time forward like man and wife, or at least that she would suffer him to lie at her house that night. But our widow, putting on a severe countenance, protested aloud that ever since the unhappy day on which her widowhood commenced, no man living had put his leg within her chaste bed, which she reserved to her lord and master, nor should do so till the rites of the Church were performed ; adding, that in her present circumstances her reputation would not suffer her to let any man, but only her nephew Augustinet, lie in her house. Don Marcos gave her his humble thanks for her civilities, notwithstanding his amorous impatience. He wished her a good repose, returned to his own lodging, accompanied by Gamara, took his end of a candle out of his pocket, fixed it to the point of his sword, lighted it at the lamp of the crucifix, and in short, did everything else that he had done the night before ; so punctual was he in every respect, unless it were that he omitted to say his prayers, because he thought his affair as good as concluded, and so did not want the assistance of heaven to further it. The banns were soon published, a cluster of holidays coming together. In fine, this marriage, so much desired on both sides, was celebrated with more expense and formality than one would have expected from so sordid a miser, who for fear of touching his six thousand crowns had borrowed money of his friends to defray the charges of that day. The chief servants belonging to his master were invited to the wedding, who all concurred in commending the happy choice he had made. The dinner was sumptuous and noble, though provided at the expense of Don Marcos, this being the first time he had ever bled in his pocket, and to do him justice, out of his excess of love he had bespoke very fine wedding clothes for Isidore and himself.

All the guests departed in good time, and Don Marcos with his own hands locked the doors and barred the gates, not so much to secure his wife, as the coffer wherein his money lay, which he had ordered to be set by his bedside. In short, the married couple went to bed, and Don Marcos, not finding all he expected, began even then perhaps to repent of his marriage : Marcella and Inez were grumbling together at their master's humour, and blamed their mistress for being so hasty to be married. Inez swore by her Maker she would sooner choose to be a lay-sister in a convent than endure to live in a house that was shut up at nine.

"And what would you say were you in my case ? " says Marcella, " for you have the pleasure of going sometimes to market to buy provisions for the family ; whereas I, who am my lady's waiting-woman, forsooth, must never peep abroad, but live a solitary life with the chaste wife of a jealous husband ; and as for the serenades we used to hear so often under our window, I now expect to hear them no more than the music of the spheres."

"Yet for all this," replied Inez, we have not so much reason to complain as has poor Augustinet. He has spent the best part of his youth in waiting upon his aunt, who has disposed of herself as you see ; she has set a formal pedagogue over his head, who will reproach him a hundred times a day with every bit he eats, and with his fine clothes, which God knows whether he came honestly by or not."

"You tell me news," says Marcella, " that I never heard before, and I don't wonder that our mistress has made so foolish a bargain on't, when her nephew *ad honores* is forced to pass his time with us. If I would have believed his fair promises, I might easily have carried off the young spark from his aunt before this, but she has kept me from my childhood, and I ought in conscience to be faithful to those whose bread I have all along ate."

"To tell you truth," continued Inez, " I have no aversion to the poor boy, and must own I have often pitied him, to see him sad and melancholy by himself, while other people are making merry and diverting themselves."

After this manner did these servants entertain each

other, and reason upon their mistress's marriage. The
good Inez soon fell asleep, but the virtuous Marcella had
other things to mind. No sooner did she find her bed-
fellow fast, but she steals out of bed, dresses herself, and
packs up in one bundle the wedding clothes of Isidore, and
some of Don Marcos's things, which she had dexterously
conveyed out of their chamber before the provident master
had locked the door. This having done, away she
marches, and because she had no design to return, she left
open the doors of the apartment which Isidore had hired
in that house. Inez awaked not long after, and missing
her companion, had the curiosity to inquire what was
become of her. She listened at Augustinet's door, not
without some little suspicion and spice of jealousy; but
hearing not the least noise there, she examined every
place elsewhere she thought it probable to find her, but
missed of her aim. At length seeing the doors wide open,
she ran upstairs, and rapped at the chamber-door of the
new married couple as hard as she could drive, whom she
strangely alarmed by this noise. She told them Marcella
was gone, that she had left the doors open, and that she
was afraid she had carried off some things, which she
never designed to restore. Don Marcos leaped out of
bed like a madman, and ran to his clothes, but found
them gone as well as those of Isidore's; when turning
suddenly about, to his inexpressible mortification, he saw
his dear spouse of so different a figure from what had
charmed him before, that he thought he should have sunk
through the floor. The unfortunate lady being awakened
so on the sudden, had taken no notice that her tower was
not upon her head. She saw it lying on the ground near
the bed, and was going to take it up; but alas! we do
nothing orderly when we go rashly to work, and in confusion she put the back part of it before; and her
visage, which had not received its usual refreshment so
early in the morning, the gloss of her paint and washes

being gone, appeared so ghastly to Don Marcos, that he fancied he saw a spectre. If he cast his eyes upon her, he beheld a terrible monster, and if he carried his sight elsewhere, he found his clothes were missing.

Isidore, who was in a strange disorder, perceived some of her teeth hanging in the large, long, and well provided mustachios of her husband, and went about in this consternation to recover them ; but the poor man, whom she had so dismally affrighted, not being able to imagine she stretched out her hands so near his face with any other design than to strangle him or pluck out his eyes, retired some paces backward, and avoided her approaches with so much address that, not being able to come up to him, she was forced at last to tell him, that some of her teeth were lodged in his whiskers. Don Marcos directed his hands thither, and finding his wife's teeth, which formerly belonged to some elephant, a native of Africa or the East-Indies, dangling in his beard, flung them at her with a great deal of indignation. She gathered them up, as likewise those that were scattered in the bed, and up and down the chamber, and then retired to a little closet with this precious treasure, her painting brush, and some other necessaries she had placed upon her toilet. In the meantime Don Marcos, after he had heartily renounced his Maker, sat him down in a chair, where he made sorrowful reflections upon his being married to an old beldame, whom he found by the venerable snow, which sixty long winters had strewed upon her bald skull, to be at least twenty years elder than himself, and yet was not so old neither, but that he might expect to be plagued with her twenty years more. Augustinet, who upon this noise had got up in haste, came half dressed into the room, and endeavoured all that lay in his power to appease the worthy husband of his aunt by adoption. But the poor man did nothing but sigh and beat his thighs with his hands, and sometimes his face. He tnen bethought himself of a fine gold chain he had borrowed to set himself off on the day of his marriage, but to complete his vexation, there was nothing but the remembrance of it left him, for Marcella had taken care to secure it among the other things she had carried off. He looked for it at first with some tranquillity, yet as carefully as might be ; but after he had wearied himself to no purpose in looking for it all over the chamber, he found it was lost, and his labour likewise, when certainly no despair could equal his. He gave such terrible groans as disturbed all the neighbourhood where he lived. Upon these doleful cries, Isidore bolted out of her closet, and appeared so much renewed, and beautiful, that the poor man thought this was the third time they had changed his wife. He looked upon her with admiration, and did not express himself angrily to her. At last he took out of one of his trunks the clothes he wore every day, dressed himself, and attended by Augustinet inquired in every street after the perfidious Marcella. They looked for her in vain till dinner, which was made up of what they had left the day before. Don Marcos and Isidore quarrelled with one another, like people that had a desire to dine, and dined like people that had as good a stomach to quarrel. However, Isidore sometimes endeavoured to bring back Don Marcos to his peaceable humour, speaking to him in as submissive and humble terms as she could think of ; and Augustinet used his best entreaties to reconcile them to each other ; but the loss of the gold chain was more to Don Marcos than a stab with a dagger. They were ready to rise from table, where they had done little else but quarrel, while Augustinet all alone by himself, employed his teeth to the best purpose ; during which there came into the room two men from the steward of the Admiral of Castile, who desired the Lady Isidore to send the silver plate he had lent her for fifteen days only, and which she had kept above twenty. Isidore could not tell what other answer to make, but that she would go and fetch it. Don

Marcos pretended the plate belonged to him, and that he was resolved to keep it. One of the men stayed still in the chamber, lest they should remove that which they made such difficulty to restore, while the other went to find out the master of the house, who came, and reproached Isidore with her unjust dealing, took no notice of the opposition Don Marcos made, and in spite of all he said to him, moved off with the plate, and left the husband and wife quarrelling about this new disaster.

Their dispute, or to speak more properly, their quarrel, was in a manner concluded, when a pawnbroker, accompanied by his porters and followers, came into the room and told Isidore that since he was informed she was married to a man of bulk and substance, he was come to fetch away the movables she had hired of him, and the money due for the loan of them, unless she was minded to buy them. Here Don Marcos lost all patience, he called the broker saucy rogue and rascal, and threatened to belabour him lustily. The broker told him he valued not his big words, that every honest man ought to restore what did not belong to him, and fell foul upon Isidore with unmannerly language, who was not wanting on her side to give him as good as he brought. He struck her, she returned the blow, and the floor was in a minute covered with the counterfeit teeth and hair of Isidore; and with the cloak, hat and gloves of Don Marcos, who interposed to defend the virtuous rib of his side.

While the combatants were gathering up their things that were fallen; while the broker removed the movables, and paid himself as honest brokers use to do; and while all of them together made a noise as if hell were broke loose, the landlord of the house, who lodged in an apartment above, came down into Isidore's room, and acquainted her that if they designed to make such a noise as that every day, they must go seek out another lodging.

" 'Tis you, you impertinent puppy, that must seek out

another lodging," replies Don Marcos, whose anger had
made him look as pale as a ghost. Upon this the landlord
answered him with a box on the ear, and our angry Don
was looking for his sword or poignard, but Marcella had
carried them off; Isidore and Augustinet interposed in the
scuffle, and with much ado appeased the master of the house,
but not Don Marcos, who beat his head against the walls,
calling Isidore a hundred times cheat, strumpet, and thief.
Isidore, with tears in her eyes, answered that a poor woman
ought not to be blamed for setting her brains to work to
get a man of such merit as Don Marcos was, and therefore
he had more reason to admire her for her wit, than to beat
her as he did ; adding, that even in point of honour, a man
ought never to lay hands on his wife. Don Marcos, swearing most heroically, protested his money was his honour,
and that he was resolved to be unmarried, whatever it cost
him. To this the meek Isidore replied with a world of
humility, that she would still be his loving wife, that their
marriage had been celebrated in the usual forms, and 'twas
impossible to dissolve it, for which reason she advised him
to sit still and be patient. When this point was pretty
well over, the next question was, where they should take
another lodging, since this was too hot for them. Don
Marcos and Augustinet walked out to find one, and in this
interval Isidore enjoyed a little breathing time, and with
the trusty Inez, comforted herself for the ill humour of her
husband, so long as she saw his trunks full of money still
in the chamber. Don Marcos took a convenient lodging
in his master's neighbourhood, and sent Augustinet home
to sup with his aunt, not being able, as he said, to bring
himself as yet to eat with such an impudent cheat.
Towards the evening he came home as surly as a baited
bear, and as fierce as a tiger. Isidore endeavoured with all
her arts to soften him into a better temper, and next morning
had the boldness to desire him to go to his new lodging and
stay there to receive the movables, that Augustinet and

Inez were going to carry to a cart which they had newly hired. Don Marcos accordingly went, and while he expected their coming, the ungrateful Isidore, the knavish Augustinet, and the jilting Inez, with all expedition conveyed the whole substance of this unfortunate man into a cart, drawn by four lusty able mules, went into it themselves, quitted Madrid, and took the road to Barcelona.

Don Marcos, who had exhausted all his patience in waiting for their coming, went back to his former lodging, found the doors shut, and was informed by the neighbours that they had removed from thence with their goods several hours before. Upon this he returned to the place from whence he came but did not find what he expected. Immediately he went back to the old place, suspecting the misfortune that had happened to him. He breaks open the chamber door, where he could see nothing but a few wretched wooden platters, an old rusty pair of tongs, a battered pair of bellows, the broken leg of a crippled andiron, and such like precious ware which they had left behind them, as not thinking it worth their while to encumber the cart with them. Now he was convinced into what treacherous hands he was fallen: he tears off his beard and hair, buffets his eyes, bites his fingers till the blood came ; nay, was sorely tempted to kill himself, but his hour was not yet come. The most unfortunate men sometimes flatter themselves with vain hopes. Thus he went to find out the fugitives in all the inns of Madrid, but could hear no tale nor tidings of them. Isidore was not such a fool as to employ a cart by which she might be betrayed, but had hired one in an inn near Madrid, and to secure herself from being pursued, had articled beforehand with the owner that he should stay no longer in the city than was sufficient to take up her, her company, and her goods.

More tired and weary than a dog that has coursed a hare and missed her, our poor gentleman was returning home, after having fruitlessly inquired at all the inns in the city and suburbs, when by mere accident he popped full butt upon Marcella. He caught hold of her by the throat, and cried out, "And have I met thee, thou traitorous baggage ? I will keep thee fast till thou hast restored every farthing thou hast stolen from me."

"Oh! good heavens," says this subtle dissembler, without changing countenance for the matter, "how did I always mistrust that this would one day fall upon me. Hear me, dear master, for the love of the blessed Virgin ; hear me, before you ruin my reputation. I am a woman of virtue and honesty, I thank my good God for it ; and should you disgrace me never so little before my neighbours here, it would be my utter undoing, for I am upon the point of marriage. Let us step a little to yonder corner, and if your lordship will but give me the hearing, I will tell you what are become of your chain and clothes. I knew well enough the blame would be laid upon me for what has happened, and told my mistress as much beforehand, when she forced me to do what I did, but she was mistress, and I a poor servant. Well, how wretched is the condition of those that serve, and what pains do they take to get a sorry livelihood ? "

Don Marcos had little malice in his nature ; the tears and eloquence of this dissembling cockatrice inclined him to listen to her, and even to believe whatever she told him. He walked with her therefore under a porch belonging to a great house, where she informed him that Isidore was an old battered strumpet, who in her time had ruined several persons that were smitten with her, but had saved nothing out of all her gettings by reason of her profuse and riotous living. She likewise told him what she had learned from Inez, that Augustinet was not nephew to Isidore but a sort of a bravo, the bastard of another whore, and that she caused him to pass for her nephew, only to give her some authority among women of her own profession and to revenge her quarrels. She acquainted him it was he to whom she had given the gold chain and the clothes that were stolen, and that it was by his order she went away in the night, without taking leave, that thereby she might alone be suspected of so wicked an action.

Marcella told all these fine stories to Don Marcos not at all regarding what might be the consequence, either to get clear of his hands, or perhaps to keep up a good old custom long ago observed by servants, which is to lie boldly, and tell their masters all they don't know, as well as all they do. She concluded her discourse with an exhortation to him to be patient, giving him hopes that his things might be restored to him when he least expected it.

"And perhaps never," replies Don Marcos very discreetly; "there is little likelihood that a traitress, who has robbed me of my goods, and is gone off with them, will ever return to restore them to me."

He afterwards told Marcella all that had befallen him with Isidore ever since she had been gone. "Is it possible she should have so little conscience with her?" says that wheedling devil Marcella. "Ah! dear master, it was not without good reason I pitied your hard usage, but I durst not say anything to you of it: for that very evening you were robbed, taking the boldness to tell my mistress that she ought not to touch your gold chain, she beat me black and blue, God knows, and called me all the whores in the world."

"But thus the case happened," says Don Marcos, fetching a deep sigh; "and the worst of it is, I see no remedy to help me."

"Hold a little," cries Marcella interrupting him, "I know a cunning man, a friend of mine, who will shortly be my husband, I trust in heaven, and he will tell you where you may find these people as plainly as if he saw them He's an admirable man, that's certain, and can make the devil fetch and carry for him like a spaniel."

The credulous Don Marcos conjured her to let him see
this son of art. Marcella promised him to do it, and told
him she would certainly meet him next day in that very
place. Don Marcos came accordingly, nor was Marcella
forgetful of her appointment, telling our unfortunate spark
that the magician she had spoke to him about, had already
begun his operations to help him to his stolen goods, but
that he wanted a certain quantity of amber, musk, and
other perfumes to make a fumigation for the demons
whom he intended to invoke, who were all of the first
order, and of the best families in hell. Don Marcos, without deliberating farther on the matter, carries Marcella to
a perfumer's shop, buys as much of those scents as she told
him would be necessary, nay, and presented her besides
with some essences and oils she begged of him, so much
did he fancy himself obliged to her for helping him to a
magician. The wicked Marcella carried him to a house
of a very scurvy aspect, where in a low room, or rather a
nasty dog-hole, he was received by a man in a cassock,
whose beard reached down to his girdle, and who accosted
him with a world of gravity.

This villainous impostor, on whom Don Marcos looked
with a great deal of respect and fear, two qualities that
generally go together, lighted two black-wax tapers, and
gave them to the affrighted Don Marcos to hold one in
each hand. He ordered him to sit down upon a little low
stool, and exhorted him, but his exhortations came too
late, not to be afraid. After this, he asked him several
questions concerning his age, his way of living, and about
the goods that were stolen from him ; and having looked a
while in a mirror, and read half a score lines in a book, he
told Don Marcos, who was ready to expire with fear, that
he very well knew where his things were, and described
them one after another so exactly to him, that Don Marcos
let the candles drop to go hug and embrace him. The
serious magician blamed him extremely for his impatience,

and told him the operations of his infallible art demanded a great deal of circumspection and care; giving him to understand, that for actions less hardy and indiscreet the demons had sorely buffeted, nay, sometimes strangled people.

At these words Don Marcos looked as pale as a criminal after sentence, and taking the candles again in his hands, sat down on his stool as before. The conjurer then called for his perfumes that Don Marcos had bought, and which the perfidious Marcella immediately gave to him. Hitherto she had been a spectatress of the ceremony, but now he commanded her to quit the room, because, says he, the devils don't like the company of women. Marcella at her going out made a profound reverence, and the magician drawing near a little pan of coals, made as if he threw Don Marcos's perfumes upon the lighted charcoal, but indeed cast a noisome composition into it, which raised so thick and dismal a smoke that the magician, who imprudently leaned over the pan, had like to have been suffocated by it. He coughed several times to expectorate the steams he had sucked in, and that with so much violence, that his long venerable beard, which was not of the growth of his chin, and had been ill-fastened on, fell down, and discovered him to be the pernicious Gamara. Don Marcos caught hold of him by the throat and gripped and squeezed him like any Hercules, crying out at the same time " thief, thief," in a shrill, terrible voice. As it happened, a magistrate was going down the street at that time, who entered the house, from whence such dismal cries proceeded that alarmed all the neighbourhood; for you must know, Gamara, whom Don Marcos held all this while by the throat, roared out as loud as he could for the heart of him. The first person the officers seized was Marcella, and after breaking open the door of this magical apartment, found Don Marcos and Gamara very lovingly hugging and tugging one another about the room. The

provost knew Gamara at first sight, whom he had been
hunting after a good while, and had ordered to be apprehended for a pick-pocket, a cock-bawd, and above all, a
notorious thief. He hurried him away to prison together
with Don Marcos and Marcella, took an inventory of all
the goods in the house, and saw them carefully locked up.
Don Marcos was enlarged, upon his master's security, that
he should appear next day. Accordingly he came as
evidence against Gamara and Marcella, who were plainly
convicted of having robbed him of his goods, that were
found safe and untouched among several other things that
had been set down in the inventory. Some of these
Gamara had stolen, and the rest were pawned to him, for he
was a Jew by religion, and consequently an usurer by
profession. When he was apprehended he was just upon
marrying Marcella, who was to have brought him by way
of portion, besides the things she had stolen from Don
Marcos, a dexterity in stealing little inferior to his, a pliant
wit, capable of learning anything that could be shown her ;
nay, even of surpassing it : and lastly, a wholesome, juicy
young carcass, considering it had been so often bought and
sold, and had endured so many heavy shocks and fatigues
in the mansions of fornication. The case appeared so
plain on Don Marcos's side, who was supported by the
credit of his master, that he had his goods immediately
restored him. Gamara was sent to the galleys for the
remainder of his life ; Marcella was soundly whipped and
banished ; and moreover, all people thought that both the
Jew and his wife elect had been too favourably dealt by.

As for Don Marcos, he was not so well pleased with
having his things again and being revenged on Gamara
and Marcella, as vexed that this great impostor did not
prove a magician. The loss of his ten thousand crowns
had almost turned his brain. He went every day to
inquire at all the inns in Madrid after those darlings of
his, and at last met with two muleteers lately returned

from Barcelona, who told him that about four or five days' journey from Madrid they had met a cart upon the road laden with goods, with two women and a man riding behind, and that they had been forced to make a halt at an inn by reason that two of the fellow's mules had been killed with being over-laboured. They described this man and the two women so well to him, and the marks they gave them so fitted Isidore, Inez, and Augustinet, that without farther deliberation he disguised himself in the habit of a pilgrim, and having obtained from his master letters of recommendation to the viceroy of Catalonia, and from the bench of justice a decree for his fugitive wife, he took the road towards Barcelona, sometimes beating it upon the hoof, sometimes on horseback, and arrived there in a few days. He went towards the harbour to take a lodging there, where the first thing that greeted his sight were his own coffers, that were carrying to a boat, with Augustinet, Isidore, and Inez attending them, which was to convey them to the vessel that waited for them in the road, wherein they designed to embark for Naples. Don Marcos followed his enemies, and threw himself like a lion into the long-boat. They did not know him by reason of his huge flapping pilgrim's hat, that eclipsed his little countenance, but took him to be some pilgrim going to Loretto, as did the seamen to be one of Augustinet's company. Don Marcos was in the strangest perplexity of mind imaginable, not so much to think what would become of him, as of his dear, dear trunks. All this while the long-boat made the best of her way to the merchantman, and sailed so swift, that Don Marcos being puzzled with what his brains were hammering, found himself directly under the vessel, when he thought himself at a great distance from it. The sailors now began to heave up the trunks, which awakened Don Marcos out of his contemplations, who always kept his eye upon the dearest of his trunks, wherein his money was lodged. A seaman at last came to take up this very individual trunk, and began to fasten it with a thick-cord that was let down from the vessel in a pulley. Now it was that Don Marcos forgot himself, for he saw his trunk tied up just by him, and did not stir ; but at last seeing it mount in the air, he caught hold of it with both hands by one of the iron rings that served to lift it from the ground, being resolved not to part with it. And perhaps he had accomplished his ends, for what will not a covetous wretch do to preserve his pelf? had not by ill fortune this trunk parted from the rest, and falling plumb upon the head of this unlucky gentleman, who for all that would not quit his hold, beat him down to the bottom of the sea, or if you please to the regions of Erebus. Isidore, Inez, and Augustinet knew him just at the very minute he sunk with the dear trunk, the loss of which troubled them infinitely more than any apprehensions they had from the revengeful Don Marcos. Augustinet, enraged at the loss of his money, and not being able to master his passion, struck the seaman, who had tied the trunks so carelessly, with all his force. The tar, in requital, gave him a heartier blow, which threw him headlong into the sea. As he fell over-board he took the unfortunate Isidore with him, who held by nothing, and so accompanied her beloved Augustinet, who against his inclination accompanied Don Marcos. Inez embarked in the vessel with the rest of the goods, which she spent in a short time after at Naples, and when she had for a long while exercised the laudable profession of a whore there, went off like one, that is to say, died in a hospital.

NOVEL II.

THE USELESS PRECAUTION.

A GENTLEMAN of Granada, whose true name I don't think fit to discover, but will call him Don Pedro de Castile, Arragon, Toledo, or what you please, courteous reader, since after all one name costs a man no more than another. For which reason perhaps the Spaniards, not content with their own names, bestow upon themselves the most magnificent ones they can think of, and sometimes tack two or three together, that are as long as a Welsh pedigree. But to quit this digression, the above-mentioned Don Pedro, at the age of twenty, found himself without either father or mother, and moreover exceeding rich ; which circumstances, when they meet in the same person, very often help to spoil him, if he be born with no great stock of brains ; but if otherwise, put him in a capacity of making what figure he pleases. During the year of mourning, he discreetly abstained from most of those diversions to which young gentlemen of his age are addicted, and wholly employed his time in taking an exact survey of his estate and settling his affairs. He was well made as to his person, had abundance of wit, and behaving himself, young as he was, with the prudence and circumspection of an old man, there was not a fortune in all Granada which he might not justly pretend to, nor a father that thought so well of his daughter but would be glad with all his heart to accept him for a son-in-law.

Among several handsome ladies, who at that time disputed the empire of hearts in that city, there was one that had charms enough to conquer that of Don Pedro. Her name was Seraphina, beautiful as an angel, young, rich, and of a good family ; and although her fortune was not altogether so great as that of Don Pedro, yet everything considered, there was no such mighty difference between them. He did not question but that at the first proposal of marriage he made to her parents he should find them ready to comply with him ; however, he rather chose to owe his success to his merit, and resolved to court her in the gallantest way, that he might make himself master of her affections before he was so of her person. His design was generous and noble, if fortune, that often delights to break the measures of the wisest politicians, had not raised him a rival, who had already taken possession of the town he designed to invest before he had so much as made his approaches. 'Tis to no purpose to tell you his name, but he was very near Don Pedro's age, and perhaps was as handsome, but all historians agree he was much more beloved. Don Pedro was soon sensible he had a competitor to remove, but this did not much alarm him, knowing few were able to dispute estates with him. He gave concerts of music in his mistress's street, while his happy rival had the pleasure to hear them in her chamber, and perhaps was revelling in her arms, while our poor lover was cooling his heels, and making melancholy reflections below.

At last Don Pedro was weary of throwing away so much powder in the mines, that is to say, of making all this bustle and courtship without advancing his affairs. However, his love did not slacken upon his ill success, but made him so impatient, that he thought fit to lay aside his first design of winning his mistress's heart before he demanded her of her friends. In short, he asked their consent, which they granted him upon the spot, without deliberating farther on the matter, being extremely pleased to be asked that which they so earnestly desired, and indeed could hardly hope for. They acquainted Seraphina with the good fortune was offered her, and prepared her to give Don Pedro a kind reception, in order to marry him in a short time. She was troubled at this news, that ought to have given her all the satisfaction in the world ; and not being able to conceal her surprise from them, dissembled the occasion of it, pretending it grieved her to part from persons so dear to her as they were. She managed this point so dexterously, that they wept out of mere tenderness, and much commended the sweetness of her temper. She conjured them to put off her marriage for four or five months, representing to them that she had been a long time indisposed, as her looks sufficiently discovered, and that by her good-will she would not marry till she was perfectly rid of her illness, that so she might come more agreeable to her husband's bed, and not give him any occasion to be disgusted at the beginning of their marriage ; and consequently to repent of his choice. 'Tis true indeed, she had looked somewhat sickly of late, which made her friends well enough satisfied with her request, and they took care to acquaint Don Pedro with it ; who, for his part, was so far from taking it ill, that he liked her the better for giving so good a proof of her discretion. In the meantime the articles of marriage were proposed, examined, and agreed on.

However, Don Pedro did not think himself excused from any of his usual gallantries, which every man is obliged to observe that courts his mistress in the common forms. He entertained her often with letters, and did not miss a day to write to her. She returned him such answers as were at least very civil, if not altogether so passionate as his own ; but she would receive none of his visits in the day-time, excusing herself upon her indisposition, and at night appeared very rarely at the window, which made Don Pedro exceedingly to admire her reserved temper. He thought too well of his own merit to doubt the success of his courtship, and questioned not to be beloved by his mistress when she came to know him better, although she should have even an aversion for him, now he was a stranger to her. Hitherto his affairs went well enough, but at last it so happened that he could not get a sight of his mistress for four or five days following. He was extremely afflicted at it, or at least pretended to be so. He composed several verses upon the occasion, I mean, either hired or bought them, and had them sung under her window.

But though he omitted nothing that the most zealous lover could practise, yet all the favour he could obtain was only to speak with her maid, who informed him her lady was more indisposed than ever. Upon this his poetic faculty was strangely perplexed, or at least the gentleman poet whom he employed ; for upon the strictest search I find versifying was never his talent. He caused an air to be made upon Aminta's being sick, or Phyllis, or Chloris, no matter whether ; and besides his offensive and defensive arms, taking a guitar with him, which we must suppose to be the best in the whole city ; he walked furiously in this equipage towards his mistress's quarters, either to make her weep out of pure compassion, or else to set all the dogs in the neighbourhood a barking, in order to complete the concert. Now any one, I believe, would say, that 'twas a hundred to one but our gentleman must do one of the two or perhaps both ; but alas! he did neither. Within fifty paces of the thrice happy mansion of his divinity he saw the door open, and a woman go out, who had much of the air and shape of his invisible angel. He could not imagine why a woman alone, and so late at night, should so resolutely turn up into a large spacious house, lately destroyed by fire. To inform himself better, he walked round the ruins, which one might enter at several places that he might get nearer the person whom he dogged. He believed this might be his mistress, who had made an assignation with his rival to meet her in this strange place, not daring to do it at home, and not thinking fit to communicate this business to a third person, which it so much concerned her to keep secret ; he therefore resolved, within himself, that in case what now he only suspected happened to prove true, he would kill his rival upon the spot, and revenge himself upon Seraphina, by giving her the most opprobrious language he could think of. Being thus resolved, he crept along as softly as he could, till he came to a place whence he could plainly see her ; for it was she, sitting upon the ground, groaning so piteously, as if she was going to give up the ghost, and, in short, after most severe pangs, delivered of a small squalling creature, which we may suppose did not give her altogether so much pain in the begetting. She was no sooner safely delivered, but her courage giving her strength enough, she returned the same way she came, without troubling her head what would become of the poor brat that she had brought into the world.

I will leave you to judge how great Don Pedro's surprise was. He now found out the true reason of his mistress's indisposition ; his head almost turned round to think what a precipice he had escaped, and he thanked heaven most devoutly for preserving him from the danger ; but being generous in his temper, he scorned to revenge himself upon the faithless Seraphina by exposing the honour of her family ; neither in his just resentment would he suffer the innocent babe to perish, which he saw lying at his feet exposed to the first dog that had the luck to find it. He wrapped it up in his cloak for want of something else, and making all the haste he could, called upon a discreet woman of his acquaintance, to whom he recommended the care of the child, putting it at the same time into her hands, and giving her money to buy it all sorts of necessaries. This discreet woman finding herself nobly paid, acquitted her charge very well. Next day the infant had a nurse, was baptized, and named Laura, for you must know it was a female.

In the meantime Don Pedro went to a relation of his in whom he mightily confided, and told her he had changed his design of marrying to that of travelling. He desired her to manage his estate for him in his absence, and to receive into her house an infant, which he said belonged to him, to spare nothing in her education, and for certain reasons, which he would acquaint her with at some other time, to send her to a convent as soon as she was three years old ; and above all, to take particular care that she should know as little as might be of the affairs of the world. He furnished her with necessary instruments to look after his estate, provided himself with money and jewels, took a faithful and trusty servant ; but before his departure from Granada writ a letter to Seraphina. She received it just at the time she had acquainted her friends that her illness should retard her marriage no longer. But Don Pedro's letter, which gave her to understand he knew what had so lately befallen her, put other thoughts into her head. She devoted herself to a religious life, and soon after retired to a convent, with full resolution never to stir thence, and could not be induced to alter her mind by all the entreaties and tears of her parents, who used all the arguments they could think of to dissuade her from this resolution ; which appeared so much the stranger to them, as they could not divine the occasion of it.

Let us leave them to weep for their daughter's turning nun, who on her part wept heartily for her sins. Let us likewise leave her little daughter Laura to grow in bulk and beauty, and return to meet Don Pedro on the road to Seville, who could not drive this last adventure out of his head, and was now as much disgusted at marriage as once he was desirous to taste the pleasures of it. He is afraid of all women ; and not considering there are both good and bad of that as well as of his own sex, he concluded within himself that a wise man ought to be diffident of all women, and particularly of the witty more than the foolish ; being, it seems, of the opinion of those worthy gentlemen, who think a woman knows more than comes to her share if she knows a jot more than stewing prunes, preserving fruits, dressing her husband's dinner, or mending his stockings.

Tainted with these heretical doctrines he arrived at Seville, and went directly to the house of Don Juan the Lord knows what, a man of wealth and quality, who was his relation and friend, and would not suffer him to lodge anywhere else but with him. The magnificence of Seville gave him a desire to make a longer stay there than he at first designed ; and his cousin Don Juan, to make his stay more agreeable to him, showed him all the most remarkable curiosities of that place. One day as they were riding on horseback through one of the principal streets of the city, they saw in a coach, that was driving towards a stately house, a young lady in a widow's habit, so beautiful and charming, that Don Pedro was exceedingly surprised, and set his cousin a laughing by the many vehement exclamations and oaths he made, that he had never seen anything so lovely in his life. This angel of a widow restored the whole female sex to his good opinion, whom the unhappy Seraphina had rendered odious to him. He desired Don Juan to go back through the same street, and frankly owned that he wanted little of being wounded to the heart by her. "Your business is done," replies the other, "and I am very much mistaken if the little god has not shot his arrow so deep, that there is no plucking it out but heart and all must come together."

"Alas!" says the amorous Don Pedro, "I will conceal nothing from you. How happy should I reckon myself if I could pass my days with so charming a lady!"

"You must go this way then," replied Don Juan, "and travelling so fast as you do, you may in a few minutes arrive at the place, where you expect to find so much happiness. Not but that such an enterprise," continued he, "will give you difficulty enough. Elvira is a woman of quality, and very rich ; her beauty is such as you have beheld it, neither is her virtue any ways inferior. During the two years of her widowhood, the best matches in Andalusia have not given her the least inclination to change her condition ; but a man so well made as yourself may perhaps succeed where others have failed. She is related to my wife, and sometimes I make her a visit. If you please, I will propose your design to her, and I have good hopes to succeed in my negotiation, since I now see her in her balcony, which is no small favour, let me tell you, in so nice and reserved a lady. She might have shut her lattices and windows, and so have balked our expectation."

These words were no sooner out of his mouth, but our two cavaliers made each a reverence after the Spanish mode, which gave them no little trouble before they could recover themselves. Especially Don Pedro made his so profoundly low, and with that contortion of his body, that he had like to have tumbled off his horse. The lady in the balcony returned them a handsome courtesy, upon which Don Pedro and his companion bowed again.

> "And when the bright charmer did leave the balcony,
>   One spurred on his horse, t'other gaped like a Tony."

"Alas! my dear cousin," says Don Pedro to Don Juan, "what probability is their that a stranger can be able to gain that heart, which has defended itself against all the men of quality and merit in Seville. However," continues he, "since my despair would otherwise give me my death's wound, I had as good receive it from her refusal and contempt. Therefore let me conjure you to speak to her as soon as you can, and don't so much enlarge upon my estate and quality as upon the violence of my passion."

Don Pedro could not talk of anything but his love, and Don Juan was sensible he could not oblige him more effectually than by taking the first opportunity to make this overture to Elvira. He accordingly did so and not without success. The charming widow received the proposal he made for his friend so well, that she confessed she did not dislike him. But withal she acquainted him, that having obliged herself by vow to stay three full years from the death of her first husband before she took a second, nothing in the world should prevail with her to break it. She added, that because she had resolved to pay this respect to the memory of her late spouse, she had hitherto refused all the offers that had been made her, but that if Don Pedro had courage and constancy enough to serve her a whole year, in which time they might know one another's tempers much better, she gave him her word to choose no other husband.

Don Juan came to give Don Pedro an account of his negotiations, and made him the most satisfied as well as most passionate of all men breathing. He was not in the least deterred by the long time he was to stay, and resolved to employ it in all the refined gallantry of a nice lover. He bought him a fine coach and horses, made his house and liveries as sumptuous as might be, set all the embroiderers and tailors of Seville at work, and the musicians into the bargain. He offered to regale Elvira, but she would not suffer it. Her servants were nothing near so difficult, for they accepted his presents as heartily as he gave them. In a short time he was more master of Elvira's domestics than she herself, whom her damsels persuaded to appear in the balcony, even when she had no mind to it, and that as often as Don Pedro exerted his lungs in the street, for I have been told he sang to admiration. Don Pedro had now spent six tedious months in courting Elvira, without being able to obtain a private conversation with her all the while, which daily increased his esteem and love for her. At last, by dint of prayers and presents, a damsel bolder than the rest, or rather more covetous, promised to introduce him one night into her mistress's apartment, and place him in a corner, where he might see her undress before she went to bed, take two or three turns in her shift to cool herself, and sing and play upon her lute, which she did to a miracle.

Don Pedro gave this trusty maid a better reward than he promised her; and when night came, our Granada adventurer, following the abigail's instruction, slipped into Elvira's house, stole up to her apartment, and there from a gallery, which was over against the chamber door, saw her lying upon a couch reading a book of devotion, whether with much attention is more than I am able to tell you, all the while her maids undressed her. She had only a light gown on, and was ready to go to bed, when Don Pedro's pensionary damsel, who designed to give him as much reason to be satisfied with her as she was with him entreated her mistress to sing. Her companions joined in the same petition; but Elvira denied them a good while, telling them she was very melancholy, nay, and assuring them she had occasion to be so. But the damsel, whom Don Pedro's presents had gained, putting a lute into her mistress's hand, Elvira was so complaisant as to sing, which she did in so charming and graceful a manner, that Don Pedro was within an ace of throwing himself at her heavenly feet, and acting there the ravished lover. The song was soon over, and then she went to bed. The maids retired to their own apartments, and Don Pedro, who made the best of his way towards the street, was strangely surprised to find the great gate locked. He had nothing now left to do but to stay there till day, which would soon appear. He sat upon the side of a well, which was in a corner of the court, strangely perplexed lest he should be discovered, and incur his mistress's displeasure for so bold an attempt. He had not been here long, but he made a thousand attempts, and wished as often, to no purpose, that he was safe in the street, when he heard a door open in Elvira's apartment. He immediately turned his head towards the place whence the noise came, and was strangely surprised to see the beautiful widow come into the court, whom he thought to be fast asleep. By the light of a wax-taper she carried in a little silver candle-stick, he saw her nightdress was nicely adjusted, her breasts open and unguarded, a fine necklace of pearl about her neck, and that over her smock, which had more lace than linen about it, she wore nothing but a rich simarre. She carried in her hand a great phial full of jelly, comfits, and conserves ; and in this surprising equipage appeared so charming, that Don Pedro had like to have preferred the pleasure of discovering himself to her, to all the ill effects which so bold a presumption might have drawn upon him. But he was wise in his love, and hid himself behind the well, though he kept his eyes upon his mistress all the while, flattering himself sometimes that it was he she came to look for. She walked directly towards the stable ; Don Pedro followed her at some distance, and saw her go into a little room.

At first he was of opinion his pious and charitable mistress went to visit one of her domestics that was sick there, though without doing any wrong to her charity she might have left that affair to any of her women. He crept behind a horse that stood not far from the chamber-door, and from thence observing his dear widow, saw her put the candle-stick and glass phial, and in short all she carried in her ivory hands, upon a little table. In a sorry bed, which in a manner took up all the room, he beheld a sick negro, who seemed to be above thirty years old, but so deformed and ghastly, that he was frightened at the sight of him. His face was as meagre as that of a skeleton, and the poor fellow had much difficulty to fetch his breath.

Don Pedro admired the unparalleled goodness of the
beautiful Elvira, who took off all the negro's blankets, and
having made his bed, sat down by the sick wretch, and put
her hand upon his forehead, that was all over in a cold
sweat. The negro cast a dismal look upon the charitable
angel that came to comfort him, and seemed to pity him
with her eyes brimful of tears. Don Pedro could not tell
what to think of so unexampled a strain of charity, and
after he had first admired it, began to alter his opinion, and
concluded it was carried too far. But as yet he had seen
nothing. The charming widow first broke silence, and
weeping at such a rate as if it were to be her last, asked the
black how he found himself.

"My dear Antonio," says she to him, in a voice interrupted with frequent sobs, "art thou then resolved to die, and
wilt thou make me die too for company? Thou dost not
speak to me, my life, my jewel. Take courage, if thou
wouldst have me live, and eat a little of this jelly for my
sake. Thou wilt not so much as afford me one kind look,
cruel creature; me, I say, that love thee, me that adore
thee. Kiss me, my dear angel, kiss me, and get well, if
thou wouldst not have me attend thee in thy death, after
I have so passionately loved thee during thy life." As she
spoke these tender words, she joined her angel face to the
diabolical visage of the Moor, which she moistened with
her tears. I fancy any man that had seen so odd a sight
would have presently thought he had seen an angel caress
a devil. As for Don Pedro, he now began to think the
beautiful Elvira as ugly as her negro; who at last casting
his eyes upon his importunate lover, whom he scarce
vouchsafed to look upon before, and with his lean bony
hand turning away her face from his, thus spoke to her in
a low feeble tone :

"What would you have me to do, madam? Will you
not let me die in quiet? Is it not enough that you have
brought me to the condition I am in, but must you force

me, now I am just dying, to throw away the little snuff of life that is left me, to satisfy your libidinous appetite? Take a husband, and expect no more drudgery from me. I will see you no more, nor eat anything you have brought me, but am resolved to die, since I am good for nothing else." When he had said this, he sunk down in his bed, and the unfortunate Elvira could not draw the least word from him in answer to all the tender things she spoke; whether he was already dead, or refused to speak to one whom he believed the cause of his death, I can't determine. Elvira wept like a church spout when it rains, and afflicted at the sad condition wherein she left her beloved negro, but much more at his unkindness, took back with her everything she had brought, and walked towards her chamber, though with so sorrowful and sad an air, that it was her great misfortune her future cuckold did not see her in that pickle. In the meantime Don Pedro hid himself in the obscurest part of stable, so confounded, that he was not half a quarter so much when he was witness of Seraphina's happy delivery. He saw this monstrous hypocrite go back the same way she came, afflicting herself like any widow at the funeral of her dear husband; and some time after hearing the great gate open, he got into the street, not at all caring whether he was seen or not, since he thought it not worth his while to have any regard for such a woman's reputation as Elvira's. However he treated her like a gentleman of honour, and did not discover what he had seen to his friend. The next day he happened to pass by Elvira's gate at the very instant the Moor was carried out to be buried. Her women told him their mistress was sick; and for four or five days following, as he passed to and fro before her windows, she was not to be seen there according to her custom, so inconsolable had the death of her lovely African made her. Don Pedro was mighty desirous to know how she fared. One day as he was discoursing with Don Juan, one of Elvira's slaves delivered him a letter from his mistress. He opened it with impatience, and read what follows.

THE LETTER.

"Two persons, who are minded to marry, don't need a third to put them in mind on't. You would persuade me you don't dislike me; and I must own, you please me well enough to grant you this moment what I did not promise you till the year was ended. You may make yourself, as soon as you please, master of my person and estate; and I request you to believe, that although I cannot deliberately embark in such an affair as this, yet your merit and my love will render it easy to me, and make me break through all difficulties whatsoever.

"ELVIRA."

Don Pedro read over this letter twice or thrice, and could hardly believe he was awake. He bethought himself that this was the second time he had run the danger of being married as ill as any man in Spain, and thanked heaven with all his heart for having delivered him from two such imminent misfortunes, by discovering to him two secrets of so great importance. As the negro's death had put Elvira upon this sudden resolution to be married, Don Pedro as suddenly resolved to get out of her sight as soon as he could. He told Don Juan that it nearly concerned his life and honour to leave Seville within an hour, and that he would only take one servant with him, that he had brought from Granada; he desired him to sell his coach and horses, and to pay his servants with the money, and conjured him not to ask the reason of so sudden an alteration and a journey so hurried, promising to write to him the very first town he stopped at. He writ to Elvira while they went to hire two mules for him; he gave his letter to the slave, and when the mules came, took the road to Madrid; being confirmed more than ever in his first opinion, and resolving to stand upon his guard against all witty women, nay, even to detest them. While he jogged gently on, full of these virtuous resolutions, Elvira opened his letter and read the following lines.

THE LETTER.

" As violently in love as I am with you, yet I always prefer the care of preserving your honour to the pleasure of possessing you. Thus you could not but observe with what discretion I always managed my gallantry. I am somewhat scrupulous in my own nature, and therefore cannot in conscience ask you to marry me so soon, since you are a widow of but a day's standing. You owe more than that comes to, madam, to the memory of the poor negro defunct, and you cannot take less than a year to lament the loss of a person who did you so considerable services. In the meanwhile, you and I shall have time enough to consider what we have to do.

" DON PEDRO."

Elvira had like to have run distracted when she read this letter, and it touched her more to the quick than even the loss of her Guinea lover had done ; but considering that Don Pedro had left Seville, and another gallant, that had all the qualifications to please her, had offered at the same time to marry her, she took him to supply the negro's room. Not but that she could have found negroes enough to have done her business, but somebody had told her there was a difference in negroes, as well as other folks, and that everything is not the devil, though it be black. In the meantime Don Pedro and his trusty mule got to Madrid, where he went immediately to an uncle's house, who received him very courteously. This uncle of his was a rich cavalier, that had an only son, that was betrothed to a young cousin that was an only daughter likewise and who

being but ten years old, passed her time in a convent, till
she came to be of age to marry him.   His name was Don
Rodriguez, and who possessed all the good qualities that
can make a man amiable.   Don Pedro entered into a
stricter league of friendship with him than men usually do
with relations, though they love them never so well ; for
they are not always our relations whom we love best.   Don
Rodriguez seemed to be disturbed in his mind, and Don
Pedro perceiving it, related all his adventures to him, that
he might oblige him by this confidence to communicate his
to him, and if he had any occasion for his service, to let
him see that he was much more his friend than his relation.
After this, he told him he had observed that somewhat sat
uneasy upon him, and therefore begged him to let him know
what it was ; otherwise he must believe his friendship was
not so hearty as his.   Don Rodriguez desired nothing more,
hoping to receive some relief in his inquietude when he had
once communicated it.   He therefore acquaints Don Pedro
that he was passionately in love with a damsel of Madrid,
who was promised to a kinsman, whom she expected every
hour from the Indies, but had never seen him, like as he
was engaged to a cousin, and waited till she was of age, of
whom he had but little knowledge.

  " This conformity of adventures," said he to Don Pedro,
" has very much contributed to increase the affection we
have for one another, although at the same time it keeps
us both in our duty whenever our passion advises us to
prefer our satisfaction to those engagements, wherein the
interests of our families have linked us.   Hitherto my love
has made as fair a progress as I could wish, though I have
not as yet been able to compass my desires, which she puts
off till her husband's arrival, when her marriage may secure
both of us from any ill consequences that may follow upon
an assignation, when we may probably do something more
than discourse and talk.   I will say nothing to you of the
beauty of Virginia, since it is impossible to say too much of

it, and because I should be apt to say so much of it that you would not believe me. However, this I am certain of, that when you have seen her and her cousin Violante, who lives with her, you will readily own, that all Spain cannot show anything more beautiful than this incomparable pair ; and when you have conversed a few moments with them, I will leave you to tell me whether you ever saw wittier women in your life."

" 'Tis this that makes me pity you," says Don Pedro to him.

"And why so ? "replied Don Rodriguez.

" Because a woman of wit," cries he, " will most infallibly jilt you either sooner or later. You cannot but know," continues he, " by the recital I have made you of my own adventures, what has happened to myself ; and I seriously protest to you, that if I could hope to find woman as foolish as I know some of them are witty, I would employ all arts to gain her, and prefer her even to wisdom itself, if she would but choose me for her gallant."

"You are much in the wrong," replies Don Rodriguez, "for I never met a man of tolerable sense in my life but was soon weary of a woman's company if she was a fool. Indeed 'tis not reasonable, that whilst our eyes, our hands, and in short all our body finds something to divert it, our soul, which is the noblest part of the composition, should be forced to endure a tiresome insipid conversation, as that of all persons must certainly be that have no wit to support it."

"Let us not carry this dispute as far as it will go," cries Don Pedro to him, "for a man may say too many things upon so copious a subject. Only let me see this miracle of a woman and her cousin as soon as you can, that if I don't dislike her, I may have something to amuse myself with during my stay in Madrid."

"I don't believe it will be worth your while," cries Rodriguez.

" And why so ? " replies Don Pedro.

" Because," says the other, " she is the only woman in the world that is least a fool."

" I will however suit myself to the time," says Don Pedro.

" To tell you the truth," answers Don Rodriguez, " I don't know after what manner Madam Virginia will receive us. For these eight days last past she has used me most unmercifully ; she has sent back all my letters without so much as opening them, and in short has given me to understand that she would never admit a visit from me, by reason she saw me some time ago talking with a young lady at church, in whose company she had seen me the same day at the playhouse ; and this is the reason why I have been of late so melancholy."

" It signifies nothing," says Don Pedro ; " let us go and see them, and take my word for it, you'll sooner reconcile matters by justifying yourself to her face, than by writing her a cart-load of whining letters."

Thus our two gentleman-cousins went to visit the two lady-cousins, and the beautiful Virginia gave Don Rodriguez leave to clear himself, which was easily done. Don Pedro thought both of them to be the handsomest women he had ever seen, not excepting either the imprudent Seraphina or the hypocritical Elvira. Violante, who had dressed herself that day in her finest clothes, because she was to sit for her picture, charmed Don Pedro so effectually, that he immediately broke the vow he had made, never to love anyone but a fool. This did not displease Violante, but he said so many pretty engaging things to her upon the occasion of her picture, that she was no less satisfied with his wit than his gallantry ; and here I am obliged to make a short digression, to acquaint those that knew it not before, that your mighty retailers of compliments and fine expressions generally deal in whipped cream, and are justly accused of bombast by men of wit and sense. If this small advice had been considered by the public, they would have found it no less useful than a receipt against flies in the summer, and stinking breaths all the year round. Don Pedro, who had solemnly sworn by his Maker that he would marry none but a fool, was now fully convinced that oaths made by gamesters and lovers signified just nothing. He was so ravished with Violante's wit, no less than her beauty, that finding he could obtain no other favours from her than such as she might grant without any prejudice to her honour, he resolved to marry her, if she did not forbid the banns. He frequently gave her occasion to explain her mind upon this article, but either she did not, or would not understand him ; whether it was because she loved her liberty, or had an aversion to matrimony, I don't tell you.

Thus all things went smoothly on between these four young lovers, and they only waited for the critical minute to consummate. One day, when these two young sparks had spruced themselves up like Castor and Pollux, and made no question to be masters at least of all the outworks they attacked, a servant maid, whose appearance boded worse luck than that of an owl, came to acquaint the two cousins that the Indian husband of the fair Castilian was arrived at Madrid, without so much as sending her advice of his coming from Seville, where he landed. The two cousins concluded from hence that he had a mind to surprise them, and therefore desired our lovers to fortify themselves with patience, till such time as Virginia had found out the humour of her Indian spark ; and in the meantime requested that they would not only forbear to visit them, but even to walk before their windows, till they received new orders. Thus all their tricking up and powdering that morning was thrown away, and the next two days they had no more mind to dress than a criminal condemned to be hanged. They learnt, among other news of the town, that the Indian and Virginia were married in private, that he was very jealous in his temper,

that he was a man of experience, having seen forty years ;
and in fine, that he had so ordered his family, and kept so
strict a watch over all Virginia's actions, that her gallants,
if she had any, must never expect to see her so much as at
her window.

The new orders, which had been promised, did not come,
and they were impatient with expecting them.   They daily
walked through the street where their mistresses lived, and
took their usual turns before the house, without seeing any
but unknown faces go in or out, and without being able to
meet with the least man or maidservant of their acquaintance.   They saw the husband go into his house one day,
accompanied by his brother, who was handsome and well
made, and so young, that he was still at the college.   This
increased their ill humour.   They went out early in the
morning, and came not home till it was very late, and lost
both their time and their labour.   At last, upon a certain
holiday, they saw Violante's maid going to mass by break
of day ; they stopped her at the church-porch, and by the
never-failing rhetoric of money, Don Rodriguez persuaded
her to carry the following billet to her mistress :

" Your forgetting me does not disoblige me, more than my
jealousy torments me, since it is without remedy, now you
are under the government of a husband.   However, you are
not totally freed as yet from my importunities, although
you have discarded me from your remembrance.   The last
favour I have to beg of you, is to inform me whether I have
any reason still to hope, or whether I must prepare to die."

They followed Violante's maid at a distance.   She delivered the letter according to her promise, and making
a sign to them to draw near, dropped the following answer
from the window into the street :

" A jealous man so newly married is never out of his wife's
company, and watches all her motions.   He talks of taking

a journey to Valladolid shortly without me ; I will then justify myself and pay my debts."

This billet, which they kissed a hundred times, by the same token that they strove which should out-do the other, gave them fresh encouragement, and made them easy enough for a few days. But at last, hearing no news from their cruel mistresses, they began after their old laudable custom to walk to and fro a hundred times a day before their windows ; they passed whole nights in the street, but could not see a soul stir out of the house, no more than if it had not been inhabited. One day, as these despairing lovers happened to be at church, they had the good luck to see our young bride come towards them. Don Rodriguez kneeled down by her, under the very nose of an old gentleman-usher that had squired her to church. He made his complaints to her in few words, she excused herself in like manner, and at last told him that her husband was not to go to Valladolid, although he daily talked of it ; that she was impatient to have a private conversation with him, and that she only knew one way of bringing it about, which wholly depended upon Don Pedro. " My husband," says she, " sleeps as sound as if he took opium every night, and we have not exchanged a word for these four or five days, by reason of a small quarrel between us, which is not yet made up. I had prevailed on my cousin Violante to take my place, but she's unhappily sick, and since none are privy to our amour but she and Don Pedro, for I would not for all the world have it communicated to more, you must even get him (if you think he loves you well enough to venture it) to supply her room, and go to bed to my husband.

" This attempt seems somewhat dangerous at first sight ; but if you consider my good man and I are at odds, as I have already told you we are, and that he does not easily wake, I don't question but it will succeed to our expectation, and this is all I can do for you." This happy love stratagem, which Don Rodriguez so earnestly desired to know, cooled him in a minute when he heard it. He not only doubted whether his cousin would take upon him to act this dangerous part, but likewise, whether he ought so much as to propose it to him. His mistress continued inflexible in her resolution, and as she took leave of him protested that in case the proposal she had made him was not well received, and executed after the manner she had directed, he had no more to hope from her; nay, she gave him full leave to banish her out of his remembrance, although at another time she would have as soon consented to her own death. Neither the time nor place would permit Don Rodriguez to talk any longer with his mistress. She went home, and Don Rodriguez repaired to his companion, who could not get a word out of him, so much confounded was he at the unhappy dilemma wherein he found himself, either to make so unreasonable a request to his friend, or else to live without enjoying that happiness which is ever more esteemed before possession than after. At length, shutting themselves up in their chamber, Don Rodriguez, after he had for a while refused to declare his grievance, opened the above-mentioned proposal to Don Pedro, gilding the pill as well as he could, to make it go down with him the better. At first Don Pedro thought he had a mind to banter him, but his cousin protesting the contrary with a very serious air, and confirming it by so many oaths, that he could no longer doubt of it, he must needs turn the thing into raillery, and therefore told him he was exceedingly obliged to his mistress for designing him such good fortune with so lovely a bed-fellow, and that it was undoubtedly the effect of Violante's gratitude, who, not being in a condition to reward his services, because she was sick, and being pressed to pay her debts, turned it over to her cousin's husband, with whom he should certainly pass the night very agreeably. He talked much to the same purpose, and jested a long while, sometimes well, and sometimes but indifferently. But Don

Rodriguez was not in a humour to be merry, for he appeared so dejected and melancholy to his cousin, that he heartily pitied him, and was afraid his despair would carry him to some dangerous resolution. Don Pedro was bold in his temper, a great lover of intrigues, and no man so ready as he to engage in any extravagant adventure ; he loved Don Rodriguez tenderly, insomuch that all this joined together made him resolve to supply the room of the beautiful Virginia, whatever her jealous husband might do to him. Being therefore fully determined upon the matter, he embraced his cousin, and put fresh life into him, and at the same time assured him he would hazard all, that he might enjoy his beloved mistress. " You will not, however," added he, " be so much obliged to me as you think. I consider it is an honourable action, whereby I pretend to get as much reputation as if I should signalize myself at a breach."

Word was sent Virginia that her proposal was accepted ; she appointed that very evening to put it in execution. The two cousins went to her house, and were introduced with as little noise as possible. Don Pedro was obliged by the fair lady of the enchanted castle to undress himself before her, being resolved that her orders should not be transgressed in the least. Don Pedro having nothing on now but his shirt, was conducted by her with all the care and circumspection imaginable to the fatal room, where opening the curtains, she softly put the bold champion between the sheets, who perhaps at that moment repented for having gone so far, and one may swear did not put himself into the middle of the bed. She went away and locked the chamber-door, which put Don Pedro into cruel apprehensions, while she repaired to Don Rodriguez, to whom I suppose she paid, like a woman of honour, all that she owed him, or at least as much as he demanded of her. In the meantime Don Pedro was in different circumstances from those of his cousin, who lay in the arms of his

charming mistress, while our too charitable and adven-
turous friend feared nothing so much as the embraces of a
detestable man, whom to his great sorrow he was like to
find a very uncomfortable bed-fellow. He then began to
consider, but it was somewhat of the latest, to what hazards
his foolish rashness had carried him. He blamed himself,
called himself fool a thousand times in his thoughts, and
was sensible that to transgress thus against any husband
was an unpardonable crime, though even he himself were
to be judge of it.

These melancholy reflections were disturbed, and his
just fears increased, by a huge villainous arm which his
bed-fellow threw over him, drawing still nearer and
nearer, pronouncing some few inarticulate words, as people
are wont to do when they are asleep, and making as if he
was going to embrace his wife. Don Pedro was terribly
affrighted, and removed this arm, that lay heavier on him,
he thought, than the greatest burthen, as gently as he
could, for fear of awaking him, and when he had so done,
with all the precaution of one in danger, crept to the bedside, thrusting half his body out, insomuch that he had
like to have fallen upon the floor, cursing his stars and his
own folly for exposing him to such dangers, to serve the
passion of two indiscreet lovers. He had hardly begun to
breathe again, when his troublesome bed-fellow laid his
leg over his; which last action, as well as the former, had
like to have made him die with fear. In short, the one
still drawing nearer, and the other getting off as far as he
could, the day appeared just at the nick when the unfortunate Don Pedro was no longer able to keep his ground
against a man who still drove him farther and farther.
He arose as softly as might be, and went to open the door,
which he found locked, a greater misfortune than any had
yet befallen him.

As he was endeavouring in vain to thrust the lock back,
it flew open all of a sudden, and had like to have broke

his nose. Virginia came boldly into the chamber, and asked him aloud whither he was going in such haste. Don Pedro conjured her in a low voice not to make such a noise, and asked her whether she had not lost her senses to venture thus the waking of her husband, and desired her to let him go.

" How ! go ? " says the lady aloud to him ; " I am resolved my husband shall see whom he has lain with to-night, to the end he may know what his jealousy has brought him to, and what I am capable of doing when provoked.' Having said this, as bold as a lioness she took Don Pedro by the arm, who was so confounded that he had not strength to get loose from her, opened the window-shutters without quitting her hold, and pulling him to the bedside, drew the curtains, and cried out aloud, " See, jealous master of mine, see whom you have lain with to-night." At this Don Pedro turning his eyes towards the terrible bed, instead of an ugly fellow with a beard, beheld his charming Violante, who had lain by his side all night, and not the jealous husband of Virginia, who had been gone into the country about eight days before.

The two pretty cousins pelted him with considerable raillery ; and never did man of wit so lamely defend or say so little for himself. Violante, who was naturally gay, and rallied with a grace, had like to have made her cousin die with laughing when she pleasantly exaggerated to her what bodily fears she had put poor Don Pedro in as often as she had pretended to be awake, and drew nearer to him. It was a long time before Don Pedro could recover out of his confusion and set his countenance in order. At last Virginia took compassion on him, and left him alone with her cousin, with whom you may suppose he had affairs of great importance to settle, because he was shut up with her till noon. From this happy hour, all the while the husband stayed in the country, the two gentlemen-cousins and the two gentlewomen-cousins met frequently together, and made the best use of their time. When the husband came to town again Rodriguez was the less happy of the two, for Don Pedro, by the charitable assistance of the servants, whom his presents had brought over to his interest, made a shift for two or three months to pass most of the nights with Violante, who was mistress of her own actions, and ever since the marriage of her cousin lodged in a separate building, which had a door into another street. He became so passionately in love with her that he earnestly desired to marry her; but whenever he made any such proposal she always turned the discourse so dexterously, that he could not positively tell whether she did it out of design or because she did not care to listen to him. In short, as there is nothing permanent in this transitory world, Violante began at length to slacken in her passion, and grew cold by little and little, insomuch that Don Pedro could not forbear complaining of it, and not knowing better how to account for this alteration, accused her of infidelity, and reproached her with having some other gallant more happy than himself. Instead of mending matters by this procedure he utterly ruined them, and made himself at last so insupportable to Violante, that she not only refused to see him a nights, but likewise to admit his visits in the day-time. This treatment did not in the least discourage him; he gained by virtue of his money one of her maids, who was so treacherous as to inform him that her mistress was passionately in love with her cousin's brother-in-law, who had just left the college; that he was a very handsome youth, and no less in love with Violante than she was with him.

To complete her perfidious treachery, this ill-conditioned devil advised him to pretend himself sick, to acquaint her mistress with his illness, and complain of her being the cause of it, which was likely enough; and in short to feign it so well, that her mistress might be no longer upon her

guard, as she had hitherto been, ever since she knew herself guilty of infidelity to him. Don Pedro played his
part to admiration. Violante fell into the trap, and our
treacherous damsel had no sooner introduced her mistress's
new Adonis, but she opened the door to the jealous Don
Pedro. He bolted very furiously into Violante's chamber,
who by that time was got to bed, and her young gallant
undressing to prepare for the encounter. He came with
his sword in his right hand towards his rival, perhaps with
an intention only to frighten him ; but our young spark
was not to be daunted so, for holding out one of his shoes
which he had just plucked off, after the same manner as
you do a pocket pistol, he aimed it at Don Pedro's head
in so formidable a manner, that he who little expected
such a welcome, and did not doubt but he would fire at
him, ducked his head, and turned the other way, which
gave our youngster time enough to get to the door.
Violante, who was desirous to break with Don Pedro,
immediately fell a laughing, and told him he was the first
man that had ever been afraid of being killed by a pistol
made of an old shoe. He was so nettled at this jest, that
he gave her a box on the ear, she took him by the beard,
they tugged and grappled, and at last the discourteous
Granada spark, after he had used her so very ill that she
had nothing but cries to have recourse to, just got into the
street at the very moment that Virginia, her husband, and
all the servants, expecting a military scuffle, came into
Violante's chamber. He immediately went to acquaint
Don Rodriguez with what had happened to him, and
without losing any more time, offered his service to the
Duke of Ossuna, who went the next day for Naples, of
which kingdom he was made viceroy. Don Pedro waited on
him to the harbour, where he took shipping with him,
leaving his dear cousin very much afflicted for his absence·
He stayed about six or seven years in Naples, being
exceedingly beloved by the viceroy, who allowed him a

considerable pension. He likewise received great returns
from Spain, through which means no one made a
handsomer figure than he, which made him be so much
the more considered in Italy, by reason the generality of
the Spaniards go thither to make their fortunes, as the
French do to spend them. He made a voyage into Sicily,
visited its most remarkable cities, and then returning into
Italy, lived two or three years at Rome, as many at Venice,
saw all the considerable towns, and at last, having been
fourteen or fifteen years out of Spain, always up to the
ears in love, or if you please, in fornication, ever a mighty
intriguer, and still confirming himself in his heretical
opinion that it was not safe for a man to marry a woman
of wit, he at length resolved to put an end to all his
rambles, and re-visit Granada, and the friends he had left
there.

What principally contributed to make him leave Italy
was his want of money, through the negligence of his correspondents, or at least he had so little left, that he had scarce
enough to defray his charges to Barcelona. He was forced
to sell some of his movables there, wherewith he bought
him a mule, and only reserved his best suit of clothes to
ride in. Thus equipped he took the readiest road towards
his dear native country, without so much as a valet to keep
him company, the servant whom he had brought along
with him from Spain being dead, as we may reasonably
suppose, of the Neapolitan disease ; and his small fund
being not sufficient to maintain another. He left Barcelona by break of day to avoid the heat and flies of the
month of August, and by nine in the morning had got
about five or six leagues. He rode through a large town,
where a Catalonian duke had passed part of his summer,
in a noble castle that faced the road. This duke was well
stricken in years, and had married a fine young lady not
above twenty years old. This day, as it happened, he was
gone a hunting, and was not expected home till the next.

The young duchess saw our Granada gentleman moving forward, from a balcony she had that looked towards the great road. His good mien made her desirous to view him nearer, besides, she was naturally very curious, and would not by her goodwill suffer any strangers to pass through her town, without sending to speak with them. Although our Granada hero could have been very willing to have travelled a few miles farther before he dined, yet could he not in good manners refuse to wait on the duchess, who sent a page to let him know she would be glad of his company. She was as beautiful as an angel ; and our Don for his part had no aversion to pretty women, although they were not duchesses. He was well shaped and tall, and the duchess took a peculiar delight. to gaze upon handsome young fellows like him, to make herself some amends for the penance she did in her husband's conversation, who was so exceedingly fond of her, and so pleased with her cheerful temper, that he thought he did not see her enough, although he was seldom from her.

Don Pedro, who was a man of wit as well as judgment, diverted the duchess extremely with the recital of his travels, and fancied at first dash that she was a lady that had no aversion to pleasure. She informed herself particularly of the gallantry of Naples, desired to know whether the women there were allowed any liberty, and whether the Italian gallants carried on their amours as bravely as those of Spain. At last Don Pedro confirmed himself by the questions she put to him, that if she did not go to the bottom of an intrigue it was not for want of goodwill. She made him dine with her, to the mutual satisfaction of both. Our Granada adventurer would have taken his leave of her after dinner, but she would not suffer it, telling him that since the duke her husband would not come home that day, she desired him to be her guest ; adding obligingly, that persons of merit were very rare in Catalonia ; and therefore whenever she had the happiness to meet them, no wonder if she coveted to enjoy their conversation as long as she could. She led him into a large closet, very cool and refreshing, adorned with fine pictures, china, and other rich furniture. It wanted not, since we are obliged to be particular, a noble alcove, embroidered cushions, and a convenient couch, with a rich satin quilt thrown over it. Here our traveller recounted to her all his adventures at Granada, Seville, and Madrid, together with those of Italy, which are not as yet come to my knowledge. The duchess listened very attentively ; at last he told her he was resolved to marry, if he could but find a woman from whom he should have no reason to apprehend any of those ill offices which witty women are always able to do their husbands.

"I have an estate," continues he, "that is far from being contemptible ; and though the woman I marry does not bring me a farthing, yet provided she has been well educated, and is not deformed, I shall make no scruple to choose her ; although to deal ingenuously with you, I would much sooner pitch upon a woman that is deformed, and fool enough, than one that is handsome and not so."

"You are certainly wrong in your notions," replies the duchess ; "but what do you mean by being well educated ? "

"I mean a woman of virtue," answered our traveller.

"And how is it possible for a fool to be a woman of virtue," cries the duchess, "if she neither knows what virtue is, nor is capable of being taught it ? Besides, how can a fool love you, that has not sense enough to know your merit ? She will trespass against her duty, without know- ing what she does ; whereas a woman of wit, although she should distrust her honour, will know how to avoid those occasions where she may run any risk of losing it."

They argued a long while *pro* and *con* upon this subject ; our Don maintaining that all the knowledge required in a woman was to love her husband, to be faithful to him, and carefully to look after her family affairs and children ; and the duchess endeavouring to convince him that a fool was not capable of doing it ; nay, though she were beautiful, would certainly disgust him at last. They mutually gave several proofs of their wit, and the good opinion they had of each other soon improved into esteem, nay, and somewhat better. Our Spaniard did not only differ from the duke in age, wit, and person, but was also one of the handsomest, best-shaped men in the world, and if he appeared such to the duchess, he likewise thought her the loveliest woman he had ever beheld.

He was as bold as a lion, and never found himself alone with a woman but he immediately offered his service to her. If she accepted it, he did his best to acquit himself ; and if she took snuff at it, would fall down on his marrow bones, and terming himself the horridest sinner in the world, ask pardon so ingenuously, and with so much hypocrisy, that the lady must needs forgive his transgression, or perhaps by way of atonement made him transgress again.

" I could never have imagined," says he to the charming duchess, " that anyone was able to make me throw up an opinion the truth of which so many experiments have confirmed to me ; but it was never yet opposed by so extraordinary a person as yourself, whose soul, without being beholden to her beauty, which however is not to be matched in the universe, may acquire her as large an empire as she pleases, over all those that have wit enough to discover that she has a greater share of it than all her sex put together. You have cured me of an error," added he, " but you leave me troubled with an illness, which is so much the more dangerous and hard to cure, as I am pleased to have it, and by suffering it to gratify the noblest ambition that a mortal is capable of having."

I cannot possibly tell how many more hyperboles he shot at the duchess's virtue, and whether he did not speak abundance of pathetical impertinences, for upon such occasions as this a man is most terribly given to be impertinent. Neither do I know after what manner the duchess received a declaration of love her gallant delivered in due form at the same time ; I mean, whether she seemed, to like it by an answer suitable to the occasion, or whether by answering nothing, she made good the old proverb, " Silence gives consent." But this is certain, that a maid of hers, who died of the king's evil in France, often owned before several credible gentlemen, that the closet door was shut for some two hours upon them, that they were together till supper time ; and although this maid, whom I suppose to have been an Andalusian, had never told me this, yet do I know full well that opportunity makes a thief. The night came, that favourable goddess to stolen love, but neither was Don Pedro nor the duchess the better for it, for partly out of good manners, and partly not to give the servants an occasion to guess, who generally do so beyond the truth, to which they have a natural antipathy, they called for candles, which were almost eclipsed by the brighter eyes heaven had bestowed upon the duchess, and which at that moment twinkled prettier than any pair of stars in the firmament. The vermilion of her cheeks was double to what it used to be, which made her appear more glorious than the sun on a fine summer's day to Don Pedro, whose visage too was a little inclined to scarlet. Thus they merrily passed away the time in exchanging glances with one another, when the servant came to acquaint the duchess that his grace her husband was below in the court. All that she could do in this surprise, was to shut up the thrice astonished Don Pedro in a large gilt cupboard, where she kept her perfumed waters, which done she put the key in her pocket, and threw herself upon the bed. The duke, who was at least threescore years old, came into his wife's closet, and found her as gay and fresh as a rose upon the stalk. He told her he had just received a letter from the king, which obliged him to return sooner than he thought.

He was very hungry, and therefore ordered the servants to bring whatever they had ready in the house into the same closet; and the duchess, who had no great stomach to eat, while her traveller perhaps wished himself ten feet under ground, took a chair near the table. She was exceeding cheerful and brisk, and of a gaiety that bestowed new youth upon her old husband, so much did it revive his spirits. It was a customary thing for her to lay extravagant wagers with him, especially when she wanted money, which her good man always took a pleasure to lose to her, being perfectly charmed with so agreeable a wife. He never fancied her more beautiful than now; she told him a hundred merry stories, by the same token, that our duke had like to have choked himself with laughing at them; for eating heartily and laughing heartily at the same time, a bit of meat happened to go down the wrong way, but heaven be praised it did him no harm.

At last the duchess, who was of a humour to turn everything into merriment, had a mind to divert herself at the expense of her gallant in the sweating-tub. Says she to the duke, " Methinks it is a long while since we laid a wager last; now I would fain lay a hundred pistoles, that I have occasion for, upon the first subject that offers itself. The duke told her he was ready, and that he would leave it to her to propose the subject. The duchess proposed several, which she knew he would not accept, and at last asked him whether he would lay that he could reckon up all the things in a family that are made of iron. The duke agreed to do it, though he thought it a very foolish thing to lay a wager on, and calling for paper and ink, so soon as the cloth was removed and his chaplain had said grace (for the duke you must know kept a good decorum in his family), he writ down the names of all the iron utensils he could think of; but it fell out luckily for the duchess that he forgot to mention a key. She got him to read over what he had written two or three times, and when he had so done, asked him if he was satisfied with it, and whether he had anything to add. She then folded the paper, telling him she would examine it at her leisure, and in the meantime relate to him one of the prettiest adventures he ever heard.

" A little after you were gone upon your sports, I was," continues she, " looking out of one of our windows that faces the high road, when I saw a man of an extraordinary mien mounted on a mule, who pricked and spurred his beast to make all the haste he could. I had the curiosity to know whither he was going in so much haste, and dispatched one of my pages to tell him I would speak with him. To be plain with you, I never in all my life saw a man better shaped, or more likely to make even a woman of virtue dispense with a conjugal vow. I asked him whence he came and who he was. He answered me so genteelly, and with so much wit, that I was desirous to have more of his conversation. So I engaged him to stay with me the remainder of the day, and to acquaint me with all his adventures, which I imagined must needs be very curious and entertaining. He performed what I desired to my expectation, and I must frankly own I was never better diverted with any history in all my life, and am resolved," quoth she, " to divert your grace likewise with it." Then she recounted to the duke all that had happened to Don Pedro at Granada, Seville, and Madrid, and her good man, who was as merry a wight as is possible for a duke to be, fell a laughing, as if he would have burst his hoops, which made the duchess and some of his chief servants, whom he allowed to be familiar with him, to join in this merry concert. After this she acquainted him with all that had befallen our Granada gentleman in Italy, which was very pleasant as I have been told, for I could never yet inform myself what the particulars were. All I know is, that the duke laughed heartily at them, and Don Pedro himself could not forbear doing the like in the chest. In short, after she had very well diverted herself with making her husband laugh, and all the company, and even Don Pedro into the bargain, who till now had had his share in the mirth, she told her husband that our traveller, after he had recounted all his adventures, was so hardy as to make love to her, and did it with so much address, that she could not find it in her heart to be angry with him for carrying his gallantry so far, and who could not but perceive that he was by no means displeasing to her. "But why should I multiply words in vain," continued the duchess; "a gentleman so well made as he may attempt anything without danger. We spent the greatest part of the day together to our mutual satisfactions, and had done so still, but that you came home when I little expected you. Not to mince matters, your return both afflicted and surprised me. My lovely stranger seemed to be in a greater consternation than myself, so I hastily shut him up in my chest of perfumed waters, from whence he must needs hear me, if he is not already dead with fear. But knowing what an ascendant I have over you, and being in my own temper incapable of dissembling even those very things where my too great freedom may do me harm, I was resolved to divert you at the expense of this poor gentleman, whom I will draw out of his hole as soon as you are gone to your own apartment, and leave him to pursue his journey to Granada, where he is going, as he tells me, to find out a woman who is fool enough, it seems, to deserve to be his wife." The duchess gave such air of probability to this true story, that the duke quitted his good humour, and turned serious all on a sudden. He looked pale, was afraid that what his wife had told him was true, and could not forbear asking for the keys of the chest, wherein, as she pretended, the stranger was shut up. She changed the discourse, and by that means increased both his suspicion and fears. He asked her once more for the keys, which she refused him. He was resolved to have them, and arose from his seat in a passion.

"Very well, sir, very well," quoth the duchess, "before you ask me for the keys in such haste, pray be pleased coolly and calmly to read over your catalogue ; you have forgot to set down keys in it, you cannot deny but that they are made of iron, and that you owe me a hundred pistoles upon the wager. Pray give them me now, as you are obliged in honour, and take notice that if I have told you a merry story, it was only to put you in mind of what you had lost, and at the same time to divert you, that you might part the freer with your money. The next time I would have you to be wiser than to take an invented story for a truth. It was not probable that so many extraordinary adventures should befall one single man, and much less that I would have told you such a story if it had been true." He laughed as if he had been distracted, admired the prodigious wit of his wife, and commended it before his servants, who were perhaps as arrant fools as himself.

"See now," cries he as loud as he was able, and laughed at the same time, "see now by what a cunning fetch the gipsy has given me to understand I have lost."

The duchess had liked to have killed herself with laughing, her woman seconded her, and Don Pedro was half dead with stifling his laughter in the chest. At last the duke, after he had ordered the steward to pay his wife a hundred pistoles, leaves her to go to his own apartment, often saying to himself that she was a true devil, and sometimes that she had the wit of a devil. The duke's servants repeated the same words after their master, so that all the while the duke was going towards his chamber you could hear nothing else upon the stairs but different voices, crying, "My lady duchess has the wit of a devil," "My lady duchess is a true devil." In the meantime the steward paid the duchess her hundred pistoles and went his way. The duchess shut her chamber-door, and having freed Don Pedro out of his little ease, who had scarce recovered of his fright, she endeavoured to convince him that a woman of wit could disengage herself with honour out of a scurvy business, the very thoughts of which would have made a fool to die with fear. She would have had him take part of a collation, which her women had just then set upon the table ; but he begged her pardon, and desired her to let him go. She gave him the hundred pistoles she had won of her husband, together with a gold chain and her picture that were worth as much more, conjuring him withal not to forget her, but to let her hear from him now and then. After this she tenderly embraced him, and put him into the hands of her maids, who let him and his mule out privately by a back-door. He did not think convenient to lie in that place, but rode two leagues farther till he came to the town where he intended to have dined the day before if the duchess had not stopped him. This odd adventure with the Catalonia duchess ran perpetually in his head. He could not enough wonder at her falling in love with him so on the sudden before she knew him, at her rashness in relating to the duke a story so nice, but so true, and last of all at her great address in applying it to her wager. He likewise admired the good temper of the duke, pitied his condition, and fortified himself more than ever in his opinion, that a woman of wit was hardly worth looking after ; and doubted not but that if the duchess had not too much relied upon the goodness of her invention, she durst never have carried on her intrigue so far nor had the boldness to communicate it to her husband. He promised himself that he would never run any such risk of being ill married, because he would either take no wife at all, or if he did, pitch upon one that was so foolish, that she should not be able to distinguish between love and aversion. As he was making these wise reflections he arrived at Madrid, where he found his cousin Don Rodriguez had inherited his father's estate, and was married to his kinswoman. He was informed by him that Violante had disposed of herself in matrimony, and that the beautiful Virginia was gone to the Indies with her husband. From Madrid he arrived at Granada. The first visit he paid was to his aunt, who welcomed him with a thousand embraces. Told him that Seraphina lived like a saint, and that her lover had died of grief, because he could not persuade her to quit the cloister to marry him.

Next day he went in company with his aunt to see young Laura, Seraphina's daughter. She had been put into a convent when she was but four years old, and now might be about fifteen. He found her as beautiful as all the angels put together, and as foolish as all the nuns that come into the world without brains, and are taken out of it in their infancy, to be buried alive in a convent. He gazed upon her, and was charmed by her beauty ; he made her talk, and admired her innocence. He now flattered himself he had found what he had been so long looking after ; and what made him take the greater fancy to Laura was that she much resembled Seraphina, with whom he had once been passionately in love, though the copy infinitely exceeded the original. He told his aunt she was not his daughter, and acquainted her with his resolution to marry her. The old gentlewoman approved his choice, and communicated the good news to Laura, who neither rejoiced nor was sad at it. Don Pedro furnished his house, and looked out for the most foolish servants he could find. He likewise endeavoured to get a set of maids full as simple as Laura, which however gave him no small trouble. He presented his mistress with the richest clothes and the finest things that Granada could afford. All the persons of quality in that city were invited to the wedding, and were as much pleased with Laura's beauty as they were disgusted at her simplicity. The company broke up betimes, and our new-married couple were left alone to themselves. Don Pedro sent his servants to bed, and having ordered his wife's maids likewise to retire so soon as they had undressed her, he shut

the chamber-door ; and now the devil put it into his head
to execute the most nonsensical frolic that ever one was
guilty of, who had passed all his lifetime for a man of sense.
He sat down in a chair, making his wife to stand all the
while before him, when he spoke the following words to
her, or others much more impertinent :

"You are my wife, and I hope I shall have reason to
bless God for it, so long as we live together. Be sure you
remember what I tell you, and carefully observe it while
you live, lest you otherwise offend God and displease me."

At these words the innocent Laura made him many
profound courtseys, whether seasonably or not, signifies
nothing, and with her two little roguy blinking eyes, looked
as fearfully upon her husband as a new-come scholar does
upon an imperious pedagogue.

"Do you know," continued Don Pedro, "how married
people ought to live ?"

"Not I, forsooth," replied Laura, dropping him a courtsey
much lower than she had done before ; "but if you'll teach
me, I'll remember it better than my *Ave Maria ;*" and
then she dropt him another. Don Pedro thought himself
the happiest man upon earth, to find more simplicity in his
wife than he durst to have hoped. He took from his
armoury a very rich but light suit of armour, which he
had worn formerly at a magnificent reception the city had
made the King of Spain. With this he equipped his pretty
idiot, put a little gilt murrion on her head, finely adorned
with plumes, girt a sword by her side, and putting a lance
into her hand, gravely told her it was the duty of all wives,
who had a mind to be thought virtuous, to watch their husbands while they slept, armed in all points as she was. She
answered him with her usual courtseys, and kept on court-
seying, till he bid her take two or three turns about the
chamber, which she happened to perform with so good
a grace, her natural beauty and military habit not a little
contributing to set her off, that our too refined politician of

a husband was perfectly charmed with her. He went to bed, and Laura continued in motion till five o'clock in the morning. Our gentleman, who was the most considering and discreet of all husbands in the universe, or at least thought he was such, got up, dressed himself, disarmed his wife, helped her to pluck off her clothes, put her to bed, which he had just quitted, and kissed her a thousand times, weeping for mere joy, that he had at last found so inestimable a jewel. He then wished her a good repose, and forbidding his servants to awake her, went to mass and about his other affairs. For I had forgot to inform the courteous reader that he had purchased a place in Granada, much like to that of our *maires*, or provosts of the merchants. The first night of their marriage passed after the manner I have related, and the husband was such a confirmed sot as to employ the second no better. Accordingly heaven punished him for his stupidity. An unlucky business happened, which obliged him to take post that very day and ride to court. He had only time to change his clothes and take leave of his wife, enjoining her under pain of offending God and displeasing him to observe exactly in his absence the duty of a married woman.

Those that have business at court, let them be as good astrologers as they please, cannot assign the precise time when it shall be concluded. Don Pedro did not think of staying there above five or six days at farthest, but however was forced to wait five or six months. All this while the simple Laura did not fail to pass her nights in her armour, and to spend her day in working at her needle, which she had learnt in the convent. A gentleman of Cordova came to Granada at this time about a lawsuit. He was no fool as to his intellectuals, and was well made as to his person. He often saw Laura in her balcony, thought her exceeding pretty ; passed and repassed before her windows a hundred times a day at least, after the mode of Spain ; but Laura let him fairly pass and repass without knowing what it meant, or so much as desiring to know it. There lived over against Don Pedro's house a poor sort of woman, but charitable in her nature, and ready to relieve the wants of her neighbours, who soon perceived both the stranger's love and the small progress he had made on the charming Laura's affections. She was a woman of intrigue, and her chief business was that of bringing good people together, for which she was admirably fitted for her trade, which lay in commodes, towers, washes, essences, elixirs, and some fine secrets for beautifying the skin and taking off freckles ; but what recommended her most for this virtuous employment was her being supposed to be skilled in the black art. She so punctually bowed to the Cordovan gentleman and good-morrowed him so often as he passed before Laura's window, that he fancied she did not do it for nothing. He accosted her, and all at once struck up an acquaintance and friendship with her ; he discovered his passion to her, and promised to make her fortune if she could but serve him in his amour. This old agent of Lucifer loses no time, gets herself introduced by the foolish servants into the company of their foolish mistress, under pretence of showing her some fine curiosities. She commended her beauty, lamented her being so soon forced to lose her husband's company, and when she found herself alone with her, spoke to her of the fine gentleman that passed so often before her window. She told her he loved her more than his life, and that he had a violent inclination to serve her if she thought fitting.

" In truth, I am very much obliged to him," replied the innocent Laura, " and should like his service well enough, but our house is so full of servants, and should any of them go away, I durst not receive him in my husband's absence. However, I will write to him about it if the gentleman desires it, and don't doubt but I shall obtain what I ask of him."

This was enough to so experienced a bawd as ours, to

convince her that Laura was simplicity itself. She therefore endeavoured to explain to her as well as she was able after what manner this gentleman desired to serve her. She told her he was full as rich as her husband, and that if she had a mind to see any proofs of it, she would bring her from him the finest jewels and the richest clothes that could be.

" Alas ! madam," says Laura, " I have so much of what you talk of, that I don't know where to put them."

" Since 'tis so," answered the ambassadress of Satan, " and you don't care that he should present you, suffer him at least to visit you."

" He may do that," says Laura, "whenever he pleases ; no one will hinder him."

" That is as much as can be desired," replies this venerable bawd ; " but yet it would be much better still if your footmen and maids knew nothing of it."

" That's easy enough," answered Laura, "for my maids don't lie in my chamber. I go to bed without their help, and that very late. Take this key along with you," continued she, "which opens all the doors in the house, and about eleven at night he may come in at the garden-door, where he will see a little staircase, that will lead him to my chamber."

This old beldame took her hands and kissed them a hundred times, telling her she was going to bestow new life upon a poor gentleman, whom she had left a dying.

"And how came that about ? " cries Laura, all in a fright.

" Why 'tis you that have killed him," replies this dissembling gipsy. Laura hereat looked pale as if she had been convicted of the murder, and was going to declare her innocence, if this wicked woman, who did not think it convenient to abuse her ignorance any longer, had not left her, throwing her arms about her neck, and assuring her the sick man would not die. You may imagine she understood her trade too well to forget the miraculous key that could open all the doors.

Some malapert critic now will fall upon my bones about this key, and tell me, 'tis all over witchcraft, and smells of a fable ; but let him know from his most humble and most obliged servant, that the gentlemen in Spain have such sorts of keys, which they call mistresses, and that in the days of yore people were better bred, and more civil than to find fault with what they did not understand. Let him maul me fore-stroke and back-stroke, all that lies within the compass of his little capacity, but I should be reckoned as great a coxcomb as he, to trouble my head any more about him. To return then to our old matron. She went to find out the impatient lover, and told him, with an infernal sneer, what progress she had made in his business. He rewarded her like a liberal gentleman, and expected the night with impatience. The night at last arrived, he opened the garden-door, and stole up as softly as he could to Laura's chamber, at the time when this silly creature was walking up and down in her room armed *cap-à-pié* with a lance in her hand, according to the salutary instructions of her extravagant husband. There was only a small light in a corner of the room, and the door stood wide open without question to receive the Cordovan gallant. But our spark seeing a person all in armour, did not doubt but he designed to get him into his clutches. His fear then prevailed over his love, as violent as it was, and away he fled faster than he had come, fearing that he should not get into the street time enough. He went to his trusty goer-between and informed her what a hazard he had run, who being mightily concerned at what had happened, went directly to Laura's house, to discourse her about the matter. Our silly innocent no sooner saw her, but she asked her why the gentleman did not come, and whether he was still sick ?

" He is not sick," replies old iniquity, " but came to wait on you last night, and saw an armed man in your chamber."

At this Laura made a long-winded laugh, then fell into a second fit, and then into a third, all which while the old woman could not tell what to make on't. At last, when she had fully satisfied herself with laughing, and was at liberty to speak, she told the reverend beldame that it was plain the gentleman was not married, and that it was she who had walked in armour in her chamber. Our virtuous matron could not tell what to make of these words, and for a pretty while thought that Laura was a downright natural, but after she had put her several questions, she came to understand what she could not otherwise have imagined, as well the great simplicity of a girl of fifteen, who ought to have known what was what at that age, as the extravagant precaution her husband had used to secure his wife's chastity. However, she thought it was best to leave Laura in her error, and instead of showing any surprise at the novelty of the thing, fell a-laughing with Laura at the great fright the gallant had been in.

A meeting was appointed that night. The old woman encouraged the gallant, and admired as well as he at the strange stupidity of our husband and wife. The night came, he got into the garden, crept up the little staircase, and found his lady again in armour, performing her conjugal duty, as she thought. He embraced her all covered as she was with iron, and for her part she received him as if she had known him from her cradle. At last he enquired what she designed to do in this armour. She fell a-laughing, and told him she durst not take it off, nor pass the night in any other equipage ; and informed him withal, since it seems he knew it not before, that it was a mortal sin to do otherwise. Our charitable wheedling Cordovan took abundance of pains to undeceive the poor creature and persuade her that she was abused, and that married persons passed their time after another manner. At last he prevailed upon her to disarm, and learn a more easy and pleasant way of performing the duties of matrimony

than her rigid husband had taught her, which Laura owned
to be a cruel fatigue. He was not long in getting off her
armour, he likewise helped her to unrig, finding she was
too long about it herself, and then threw himself into the
bed by her side, where he made her confess that chalk
and cheese were not more different than his precepts of
matrimony, and those of her husband. In short, he taught
Laura all he knew, who for her part was not backward to
learn, while her husband danced attendance at court. At
last she received a letter from him, wherein he sent her
word that, his business being now over, he was preparing
to come home : and at the same time our Cordovan having
dispatched his affairs at Granada, returned to Cordova,
without so much as taking leave of Laura, being, as I
suppose, not very much concerned to part with her, since
nothing is so short-lived as our love for a fool.

Laura was not much mortified at it, and received her
husband with as much joy, and as little concern for the
loss of her gallant, as if she had never seen him. Don
Pedro and his wife supped together, to their mutual
satisfactions. The night was now pretty well spent : Don
Pedro went to bed according to custom, and you may
judge what a surprise he was in when he saw his pretty
consort in her smock coming to lie by him. Being much
disturbed in his righteous spirit, he asked why she was not
in her armour.

"Oh," says she, "I now know a much better way of
passing the night with one's husband, which my other
husband taught me, I thank him."

"What, have you got another husband then ?" replies
Don Pedro.

"Yes," says she, "and so fine and handsome a husband
too, let me tell you, that you'd be pleased to see him ;
but in truth I don't know when we shall see him again, for
ever since the last letter you sent me he has not been
here."

Don Pedro dissembling his vexation, asked her who he was ? but she could not resolve him, and like a loving tit proposed to Don Pedro to show him what a pretty game her other husband had taught her. Our unfortunate gentleman pretended to be sick, and perhaps was really so, at least in mind. He turned his back, and chewing the cud upon the blessed choice he had made of a wife, who had not only violated the honour of his bed, but had not sense enough to conceal it from him, bethought himself of the wholesome advice of the Catalonian duchess, detested his errors, and owned (but it was somewhat of the latest,) that a woman of wit knows how to preserve the laws of honour ; or if out of weakness she breaks them, knows at least how to keep her transgression private. At last he comforted himself as well as he could for a calamity that was not to be redressed : he feigned to be indisposed for some time, to see whether the instructions of his deputy would have any other effect than just teaching her a lesson, which he had done better to have taught her himself. He lived several years with her, had always a watchful eye over her actions ; and when he died left her all his estate, upon condition she would take upon her the habit of a nun, in the same convent where Seraphina lived, who was at the same time informed by him that Laura was her daughter. He sent all the particulars of this history to his cousin Don Rodriguez at Madrid, and confessed to him how finely he had found himself mistaken in his erroneous opinion. He died ; Laura neither rejoiced nor grieved at his death. She entered herself in the same convent where her mother lived ; who finding what a great estate Don Pedro had left her daughter, founded a religious house with it. The history of Don Pedro was divulged after his death, and convinced all those people, who doubted of it before, that virtue cannot be perfect without good sense ; that a witty woman may be honest of herself, but that a fool cannot be so without assistance and good looking after.

NOVEL III.

THE HYPOCRITES.

IT was in that lovely season of the year, when Flora and Apollo—no, I beg your pardon, Apollo and Flora—dress the earth in her gayest livery, that a woman arrived at Toledo, the most ancient and most renowned city of Spain. She was fair and young, as subtle as the old serpent, and so great an enemy to truth, that for several years she never suffered that virtue to approach her lips; and what is more wonderful, did not find herself a jot the worse—at least she never complained of it. Thus she trafficked in lies, and generally made a good market of them; for nothing is more certain, than that a cheat of our heroine's complexion has sometimes stole herself into the approbation even of those persons who have a mortal aversion to falsehood. She had a magazine of fiction large enough to furnish all the poets, heralds, vision-mongers, quacks and astrologers in Christendom. In short, this natural qualification, which she had taken care to cultivate from her infancy, joined to the charms of her face, had got her in a short time a fine parcel of pistoles. Her eyes were black, lively, brilliant, large, as fine as fine could be, but withal most notorious killers, convicted of some four or five murders, suspected of fifty more that were not sufficiently proved ; and as for the wretches they had wounded, their numbers could not be computed, nor even imagined. No woman in the universe dressed finer; the least pin fixed by her hand carried a peculiar charm with it. She advised with no other counsellor as to her dress than her looking-glass, which was her chief minister of state, her treasurer, and father confessor. She was a most dangerous woman to look upon, that's certain; for a man could not for the heart of him help loving her, and yet could not be long her gallant, without being her slave as long.

Well, our lady, such as I have described her, arrived at Toledo towards the evening, just at the very nick when all the cavaliers of the city were preparing a masquerade for the wedding of a young gentleman of the neighbourhood, who was to marry a lady descended of one of the best families in that city. The windows were illuminated with torches, but much more with the brighter eyes of the fair ladies, and the incredible number of wax lights triumphed o'er the vanquished night, and restored the foregoing day. Women of the least quality showed all their finery upon this occasion. A world of beaux had most nicely spruced up their fine persons with a felonious intention to murder the ladies. I mean those empty fops that all great cities are plagued with, who don't care a farthing whether they make real conquests or not, provided they can but have the reputation or scandal of them : who never attack but in a troop, and that always with insolence, and who by virtue of a handsome face, red stockings, a gilt snuff-box, and a fine periwig, think they can command the lives of all they meet, and murder all the women with love and all the men with fear. Oh! what a fine time had the men of compliment that day to show the fruitfulness of their imaginations ; and how much glittering rhetoric was thrown away upon goddesses, who had not been deified a full hour. Among the rest a dapper younker, who from a school-boy had advanced himself to the dignity of a page, surpassed himself in talking magnificent nonsense before our heroine, and never was better pleased with his dear person than then. He had seen her alight out of the stage coach, by the same token he was terribly smitten with her ; but resolving not to stop there, followed her to the very door of the house where she hired a room, and from thence to all the several places where her curiosity led her. At last our stranger stopped at a certain place, where she might behold the masks at her ease ; and our eloquent page, who had put on his best linen that day, and was finer than ordinary, immediately entered into a conversation with her, and began to display his talent. She was a woman that understood the world very well, and loved dearly to banter and laugh at your forward young prigs, that think they are born with a patent to be troublesome. Judge therefore if, finding our page an everlasting talker, that cared not what came uppermost, she did not soon carry the shallow sot out of his depth, and manage him as she pleased. She intoxicated him with her praises, so that both his heart and soul were at her service. He told her that he waited on an ancient cavalier of Andalusia, uncle to the young gentleman that was to be married, for whom the city made all this rejoicing ; that he was one of the richest men of his quality, and that he had no other heir but this young nephew, whom he loved exceedingly, although he was one of the most extravagant young fellows in Spain, a lover of all the women he saw, and, besides, of a little army of whores and other women whom he had in-veigled, either by fair speeches or money ; and lastly, that he had committed several rapes, without respect either to age, degree, or condition. He added, that his follies had been very expensive to his old uncle ; who was the more desirous to link him in matrimony, that he might see whether he would not alter his manners with his condition. While the page discovered all these affairs and secrets of his master, she made him giddy with her flatteries, commending every word he spoke, bidding the company to observe

with what a grace he told his story ; and, in short, omitting
nothing that might help to turn the head of a young fop.
who had already but too good an opinion of his own parts.

The commendations and applauses that proceed from a
fair mouth are dangerous and deceitful. Our indisceet
page had no sooner informed Helen that he was a native
of Valladolid but she began to express herself very much
in favour of that city and its inhabitants ; and after she
had put herself to the expense of some hyperboles in
praising them, assured our young coxcomb that of all the
fine gentlemen she had known of that country, she never
yet saw one so well made and accomplished as himself.
This was the finishing compliment, that pinned up the
basket. Just as our page was going to take his leave of
her, she invited him to conduct her to her lodgings, and
you must not ask the question why she gave her lily-white
hand to him rather than another. This unexpected favour
made his heart to leap within him, so that he was perfectly
out of his little senses ; and he concluded within himself
that a man ought not to despair of his good fortune, although
he were never so miserable. When our charming flatterer
came into her room, she placed the page in the best seat.
He was so confounded at this kind treatment, that for
want of taking due care, he came souse with his breech to
the ground : his cloak fell one way, his hat and gloves
another, and besides, he had like to have run himself
through with his poignard, which dropped out of the
scabbard as he fell. Helen went to help up our poor spark,
and seemed to be mightily concerned at his mischance. She
put up his poignard and told him she could not see him wear
it any more that day, after the slippery trick it had played
him. The page picked up the scattered remains of his shipwreck, and made several wicked compliments suitable to
the occasion. All this while Helen made as if she could
not recover herself from her late fright, and began to
admire the fine workmanship of the poignard. The page

gave her to understand it belonged to his old master, who had formerly bestowed it upon his graceless nephew, with a sword and other accoutrements belonging to it, and that he had chosen it among several more, that were in his master's wardrobe, on purpose to make a better figure upon a day of such public solemnity.

Helen made the page believe she had a mind to go out in disguise, to see after what manner people of quality were married at Toledo. The page told her the ceremony would not be performed till midnight, and offered her a small collation in the apartment of the master of the house, who was his friend. He railed at his unpropitious stars, that he was forced to quit the most agreeable company in the world to wait upon his master who kept his bed by reason of his illness. He added, that his gout was the reason why he did not assist at the wedding, which was to be kept in a great house in the city, at a good distance from his own, that was called the hotel of the Count of Fuensalida. He was pumping his brains to make some pretty compliment at parting, when he heard somebody knock very hard at the door. Helen seemed to be strangely discomposed at it, and desired the page to retire into a little closet, where she shut him up longer than he imagined. He that made such a rapping at the door was Helen's gallant, half pimp and half bully, whom, to stop the mouths of the wicked, she was pleased to call brother. He was the trusty accomplice of all her rueful actions, and drudge in ordinary to her private pleasures. She told him how she had disposed of the page, and discovered to him besides her design to finger some of his old master's pistoles, which required as much speed as dexterity in the execution. The mules, though very well harassed, were immediately put into the coach that had brought them from Madrid; when Helen with her company (which was composed of the terrible Montafar, the venerable Mendez, and a small lackey) embarked in this foundered vessel, which carried them to a sort of Long Lane, where a parcel of

Christian Jews lived, whose faith was as threadbare as the
secondhand clothes they sold.   The maskers ran still about
the streets ; and it so happened, that the bridegroom, who
was masked as well as the rest, met Helen's coach, and in
it beheld our dangerous stranger, who seemed to him to be
Venus in disguise, or the sun hurrying about the streets.
He was so strangely tempted by this bewitching sight,
that he was within an ace of leaving his bride elect in the
lurch to run after this unknown fair ; but at that time his
prudence had power enough to stifle this growing passion,
he followed his companions in the masks, while the stage-
coach drove furiously on towards the aforesaid street, where
the brokers lived, and here, without much haggling and
making of words, Helen soon equipped herself in mourning
from top to toe, together with the ancient Mendez,
Montafar, and the little boy.

   After this, getting into the coach again, she ordered the
fellow to stop at the hotel of the Count Fuensalida.   Our
diminutive lackey went in first, enquired out the apartment
of the Marquis of Vallafagnan, and told him that a lady
from the mountains of Leon was at the door, who had some
business of great importance to communicate to him.   The
good gentleman was surprised to hear of a visit from such
a lady, and at such an hour : he raised himself up in his
bed as well as he could, adjusted his wrinkled cravat,
and ordered two cushions to be put under his back, to
receive so important a visit with the better grace.   He kept
himself in this posture, with his eye still fixed upon the
chamber-door, when he saw enter the room (not without
the greatest admiration of his eyes, and as great a palpitation of his heart) the sorrowful Montafar, muffled up in as
much black crape as would serve half a score hearses,
followed by two women in the same habit, the youngest of
whom he led by the hand, and who covering part of her
face with her veil, seemed to be the most sorrowful and
considerable of the two.   A lackey held up her train, which

was so enormously prolix, that when it was spread out it covered the whole floor. At the door they saluted the sick old gentleman with three profound reverences, not reckoning that of the little lackey, which is not worth mentioning. In the middle of the room with three other reverences all at the same time, and three more before they took their seats, which were brought them by a young page, comrade to him whom Helen had locked up safe in the closet ; but these three last reverences were so extraordinary, that they effaced the remembrance of the former.

The courteous soul of our old gentleman was strangely surprised at so odd a scene, the ladies took their seats, and Montafar and the little lackey retired bare-headed towards the door. The gouty cavalier was at his wits' end to find them compliments, and afflicted himself at their mourning before he knew the cause of it, which he entreated them to be so kind as to let him know, as likewise the reason why they did him the honour of that visit at so unusual an hour for persons of their quality to be abroad. Helen, who needed not to be informed what a strange efficacy and persuasion there was in tears that came from beautiful eyes immediately poured out a torrent of them, intermixed with violent sobs and sighs raising and falling the tone of her voice as she saw most proper. She discovered ever and anon her lily-white hands, with which she wiped her eyes, and sometimes showed her face, to let him see she was as beautiful as afflicted. The old gentleman expected with impatience when she would open, and began now to hope it since that impetuous flood of tears, which had overflowed her charming field of lilies and roses, was in a manner stopped ; when the venerable Mendez, who judged it convenient to reassume this mournful harmony, which the other had just finished, began to weep, sob, and lay about her with that violence, that it was equally a misfortune and shame to Helen that she had not grieved enough. The old matron stopped not here, but resolving to outdo Helen, thought that to tear off a handful or two of her hair would not have an ill effect upon the audience. It was no sooner thought of but done : she committed most horrible ravage upon her locks, but in truth this was no mighty loss to her since there was not one single hair of the growth of her head.

After this manner did Helen and Mendez strive who should exceed the other, when Montafar and the lackey, at a signal concerted between them, began a doleful concert at the door, and wept and sighed so cruelly, that one would have thought they had designed to outrival the two pensive ladies near the bed ; who by this new striking up of the chorus, began to play their parts again so furiously, as if they had been too remiss before. The old gentleman was almost distracted to see them weep so immoderately, and yet could know nothing of the occasion. He wept however to keep them company, sobbed as strenuously as the best of them, and conjured the afflicted ladies by all that was good and sacred, by their seraphical eyes, and their celestial charms, to moderate their afflictions a little, and to acquaint him with the cause of them ; protesting, that his life was the least thing he would hazard for their sakes, and regretting the loss of his youth, which hindered him from showing the sincerity of his heart by his actions.

At these words the sky began to clear up a little, their countenances were not so overcast as before, and they thought they had wept enough in all conscience, since they could weep no longer without spoiling the jest. Besides, they were good husbands of their time, and knew that they had not a minute to lose. Our old matron therefore, lifting up her veil above her head, to the end her venerable looks might give her all the credit she wanted on this occasion, declaimed in the following manner. " God of His Almighty power and goodness preserve and shield my Lord Marquis of Villafagnan from all harm, and restore him to his former health. Although, to speak truth, the tragical story we are going to tell him is not very proper to give him joy, which is the elixir of health : but our misfortune is of that nature, that we must communicate it."

At this the poor Marquis of Villafagnan, striking himself with the palm of his hand upon his thigh, and fetching a deep sigh from the bottom of his heart, cried, "Heaven grant that I am mistaken, but my foreboding mind tells me that this is some foolish frolic, or rather some extravagance of my nephew. Go on, madam, go on, and excuse me for interrupting you."

Our old matron fell a-weeping, instead of returning an answer, when the pensive Helen took up the discourse thus : "Since you know by sorrowful experience," says she "that your nephew is a slave to his extravagant appetites, and have been but too often troubled to compound his outrages, you will make no difficulty to believe his brutal usage of me. When you unhappily sent him to Leon last spring, he saw me at church, and at this interview said some things to me which, had they been true, neither of us ought to have stirred off from that holy ground ; myself, for fear of justice, as being his murderer, and he as a dead man and fit to be put in his grave. He told me a hundred times that my eyes had killed him, and omitted none of those insinuating wheedling tricks that lovers employ to abuse the simplicity of poor virgins. He followed me home to my lodgings, rode before my windows every day, and serenaded me every night. At last, finding all his amorous arts signified nothing, he by his money corrupted a black wench, a slave of ours, to whom my mother had promised her liberty, and by her infernal treachery surprised me in a garden we have in the suburbs of the city. I had none but this perfidious maid with me : he was accompanied by a man as wicked as himself, and had bribed the gardener to go to the other end of the town under pretence of business. What need I say more ? he clapped his poignard to my throat, and finding that my life was less dear to me than my honour, by the help of the companion of his crime, he took that by force which he could never have obtained by fair promises. The black acted the part of a distracted woman, and, the better to hide her perfidy, wounded herself slightly in the hand, and then vanished. The gardener returned : your nephew, affrighted at the blackness of his crime, leapt over the garden wall with so much precipitation, that he dropped his poignard, which I took up. However, this insolent young man had nothing then to fear ; for not being in a condition to stop him, I had command enough over myself to dissemble the inexpressible misfortune that had befallen me. I did all I could to appear no more concerned than I used to be. The wicked slave was not to be seen from that moment.

"Soon after I lost my mother, and I might say I lost everything in her, if my aunt, whom you see there, had not been so kind as to take me to her own house, where she makes no difference between her two beautiful daughters and myself. There I came to be informed, that your nephew was so far from designing me reparation for the injury he had done me, that he was upon the point of marrying in this city. Upon this I flew hither with the greatest haste I could, and expect, before I go out of your chamber, that you will give me in money or jewels, the value of two thousand crowns, to settle me in some convent ; for after what I have known by fatal experience of the temper of this cavalier, I can never bring myself to marry him, although he and all his relations should endeavour to persuade me to it by all sorts of offers and entreaties imaginable. I know well enough that he is to be married to-night, but I'll soon stop all proceedings, and raise such a hurricane, as shall make his heart ache as long as he lives, if you don't comply with my proposal. And to let you see," continued this dissembling hypocrite, "that what I have told you of your nephew is so true, that nothing can be more, see the fatal poignard which he clapped to my throat ;

and would to God he had done something more, than only threatened me with it."

She began to weep afresh at the conclusion of her story. Mendez took it in a higher key, and the harmonious concert at the door, of which the little squeaking lackey made the treble, and Montafar the bass, tuned their pipes to admiration. Our old gentleman, who had already but too easily believed what the greatest cheat of her sex had told him, no sooner saw the poignard, but he immediately knew it to be the same he had formerly bestowed upon his nephew. Therefore all his care was to prevent this story's taking air, lest it should hinder his match.

He would have sent for him with all his heart, but he was afraid lest some people should be so curious as to enquire into the occasion ; and as 'tis natural for us to fear, where we desire, he no sooner saw our afflicted ladies rising from their seats, and making as if they were going to break this marriage to pieces, which he so earnestly desired, and had taken so much pains to bring about, than he ordered his page to bring him his cabinet, and bid him tell out two thousand crowns in four pistole pieces. Montafar received them, counting them one by one ; and the old marquis having made them promise to honour him with a visit next morning, excused himself a hundred times to the ladies, for not being able to wait upon them to their chariot. Away they went very well satisfied with their visit, and ordered the coachman to drive back to Madrid, concluding with themselves, that if they were pursued, it would be on the road to Leon. In the meantime their landlady finding her lodgers did not come home, went into their chamber, where she found the page in the closet, who could not imagine why they had shut him up there, and whom she let go about his business, by reason she knew him, or rather because upon enquiry she found none of her movables missing. Those people that make a trade of robbing, and wholly subsist by it, though they don't fear God, yet always fear man. They are of all countries, and yet are of none, as having no settled habitation. As soon as they set foot. in one place, they make the most on't they can, and when they have grazed it bare, remove to fresh quarters. This cursed occupation, which is learnt with so much pains and danger, differs from all others in this respect, that whereas we leave the rest when we grow old, purely for want of strength to follow them, that of robbing generally leaves a man in his youth, and yet 'tis for want of living longer. One would think that the gentlemen that follow it must needs find some unaccountable charms in it, since for its sake they venture a great number of years, which are sooner or later concluded by the hangman.

Helen, Mendez, and Montafar, had none of these pious reflections in their heads, but rather were in perpetual fears lest they should be pursued. They gave the coachman double his fare to make the more haste, who, without question, did all he could to please his passengers that had paid him so liberally ; so that we may reasonably conclude, never did any leathern vehicle make more haste to Madrid. Montafar was very uneasy, and showed by the many sighs that escaped from him, that he was rather in a penitential than a merry strain. Helen, who had a mind to divert his melancholy by recounting the particulars of her life, which till that moment she had carefully concealed, began thus :

"Since I find thou art in such a musty humour," said she to him, " I will satisfy the great longing thou hast always expressed to know who I am, and what adventures have befallen me before we came acquainted. I could tell thee I am descended from a noble family, and, according to the vanity now predominant, give myself an illustrious name as easily as any of my neighbours ; but I will be so sincere, as to acquaint thee, even with the least faults of those who sent me into the world. You must know then, my father, of happy memory, was a Gallician by birth, a lackey by profession, or to speak more honourable of him, a footman. He held the memory of the patriarch Noah in singular veneration, for his noble invention of the vine ; and were it not for his particular respect to the juice of the grape, one might say of him that he cared but little for the vanities of this wicked world.

" My mother was of Granada, to speak frankly, a slave ; but you know there's no contending with one's destiny. She answered to the name of Mary, which her masters gave her at her baptism ; but was better pleased to be called Zara, which was her Morisco appellative : for since I am to tell you the truth, the whole truth, and nothing but the truth, she was a Christian in complaisance and fashion only, but a Moor in reality. Nevertheless she frequently confessed, but that rather the sins of her master than herself ; and as she amused her confessor not with her own failings, but the things she was forced to suffer as a servant, and showed him of what a meek, humble, and patient spirit she was, the charitable old father, who was a godly man, and judged of others by himself, believed her upon her word, and commended instead of reproving her, so that any one that stood near enough, would have heard nothing but praises on both sides. Perhaps you are in pain to know how I came acquainted with so particular a secret, and may very well imagine my mother never disclosed it to me : but I must inform you, that I am very inquisitive in my nature, and as young as I was at that time, my mother never confessed herself, but I got as near as I could to overhear her confession. But to proceed, as tawny, or to express myself more properly, as black as she was, her face and shape were not disagreeable, and there were more than six cavaliers, commanders with red and green crosses, that were her humble admirers, and strove who should be most in her good graces. She was of so charitable a temper, that she granted them all they asked of her, and her gratitude to her masters was so great, that to make them some amends for the pains they had been at in rearing her from her childhood, she did all that lay in her power to bring them every year a little slave, male or female : but heaven did not second her good intentions, for all her motley progeny, her chequered issue, I mean all the squalling demi-negroes of her making, died as soon as they were born. She was happier in bringing up the children of other people. Her masters that had lost all their own in the cradle, got her to nurse a young child, despaired of by the physicians, who in a short time, by her good looking after it, and the good qualities of my mother's milk, was perfectly recovered. For this piece of service, my mother's mistress gave her her liberty when she died. Being now at her own disposal, she set up for washing and whitening of linen, and succeeded so well that way, that in a short time there was hardly a beau or courtier in Madrid, that thought his linen well washed unless it had passed her hands.

"And now she began to practise over those lessons again which her mother had formerly given her, I mean to renew her acquaintance with her correspondents in the other world. She had laid aside this ticklish employment rather out of modesty, and because she was tired with the encomiums that were given her for being so well skilled in this art, than for any fear of justice, or apprehension of the magistrate. In short, she applied herself afresh to it, only to oblige her friends, and in a little time made so great a progress in this noble science, and acquired such credit in the kingdom of darkness, that demons of the highest reputation were not thought to be worth a farthing if they were not in league with her. I am not vain, neither do I love to tell lies," added Helen ; "for which reason I will not bestow any good qualities upon my mother which she did not possess, but am obliged at least to pay this testimony to her virtue. The secrets which she told, those which she revealed, and her oracles, which made her pointed at in the streets, were vulgar talents among those of her nation, in comparison of what she knew in the mystery of maiden-heads. That incomprehensible flower was much better after she had lent it a lifting hand, than before it was gathered, and bore a greater price as its second edition, with my mother's corrections and amendments, than at the first.

"She might be about forty years old when she married my father, the good Rodriguez. All the neighbourhood wondered a man who loved wine so well would marry a woman that never tasted it, as if she still continued a disciple of Mahomet, and who had her hands always in water, being a laundress by profession. But in answer to this, my father worthily replied that love cleared all diffi-culties, and made everything easy. Some time after, her belly swelled to her chin, and she was happily delivered of me. But this joy did not last long in our family. I was about six years old, when a certain prince clothed a hundred lackeys in his own livery against a bull-feast. My father was one of the number, drank a large morning's draught, and being pot-valiant, must needs encounter a wild bull, who tossed him two or three story high, and tore out his guts. I remember they made ballads upon my father's death, and the burthen of the song was, 'That two of a trade can never agree.' I did not understand the meaning on't then, but have since been informed, that it alluded to his being a cornuted animal ; but you know 'tis impossible to stop people's mouths, if they have a mind to prate, and vent their ill-natured mirth. My mother was afflicted at my father's misfortune, and so was I ; she was comforted, and so was her daughter. When I was grown up, my beauty began to make people talk of me ; and lord ! what pressing and thronging there was to carry me to the park, to the play-house, and to give me collations on the banks of the Manzanares.

"My mother watched me like a second Argus, insomuch that I grumbled to be so confined ; but she soon made me sensible it was for my advantage. Her severity, and the high price she set upon me, enhanced the value of her merchandise, and raised a terrible competition among those that pretended to my favours. I was as it were put up by auction, each man thought he had the better of his rival, and each fancied he had found that which was long gone and vanished. A rich Genoese merchant, who courted me in private, so dazzled the eyes of my prudent mother with his yellow metal, and bled so plentifully, that she favoured his good intentions. He possessed the first place in my affections, but this superiority proved very expensive to him. We continued faithful to him so long as we believed he doubted us: when we found him no longer upon his guard, we fairly duped him. My mother was too tender-hearted and sensible of the pains of love, not to be touched with the continual complaints of these gentlemen, who were all topping cards at court, and as rich as Crœsus. 'Tis true, they did not throw their money about so plentifully as the Genoese, yet my mother, as she knew how to set a value upon great gains, so did not despise the smaller; and besides, was obliging rather out of a principle of charity than interest. The Genoese in short was declared bankrupt, and I don't know but we might lend a helping hand to his breaking. He was engaged in several scuffles and quarrels about me. The magistrates came to visit us more out of civility than any other reason; but my mother had a natural aversion to the gentlemen of the long-robe, and no less hated your bullies and rakehelly red-coats that began to besiege us. She therefore thought convenient to remove to Seville, turned all her plate and furniture into ready money, and took me along with her in the stage-coach. We were betrayed by our villainous coachman, robbed and stripped of all we had, and besides my mother was so bruised and battered, by reason she defended her own goods as long as her little strength would give her leave, that before I could drag her to a wretched inn, she gave up the ghost at the foot of a rock. I armed myself with resolution, although I was but very young. I bundled up every rag belonging to the old gentlewoman, but our thieves had been so careful, that they had left me but little to carry off. Thus I left her to the discretion of the next passengers, not doubting, but that upon so great a road as that between Madrid and Seville, some charitable Christians would come by, and take care to see her corpse interred. I arrived at Madrid ; my lovers were acquainted with my misfortune, and in a short time I was equipped with new rigging and furniture. About that time I happened to meet with thee at one of my female companion's, and I was perfectly charmed with thy good qualities. What has happened since I need not relate to thee, since we have never been asunder. We came to Toledo ; we left it in haste, but made so good a market there, that if thou art a man of that courage I take thee to be, thou wilt be merrier than thou art. But since this long story has made thee inclinable to take a nap, as I find by thy yawning and nodding thou art, lay thy head upon my lap and sleep ; but know, that if there is anything either good or useful in fear, 'tis before we have committed a crime, for 'tis the vilest and most dangerous quality in the world afterwards. Fear always discomposes the minds of the guilty, in such manner, that instead of flying from those that pursue them they frequently throw themselves into their hands."

Montafar fell asleep, and the morning awaked, so beautiful and charming, that the birds, the flowers, and fountains saluted her each after its manner ; the birds by singing, the flowers by perfuming the air, and the fountains by smiling or murmuring, no matter which, for one is as true as the other. And now the nephew of the Marquis of Villafagnan, the sensual Don Sancho, was getting up from his new bride, tired enough in all conscience, and perhaps already glutted with the pleasures of matrimony. He could think of nothing but the pretty stranger, I mean the dangerous Helen, whom he had seen the night before in the stage-coach, and fancied to be the Phœnix of her sex ; but in which particular he was guilty of great injustice to his own lady, who was very beautiful, and so amiable, that several lovers in Toledo died for her, while at the same time she sighed for her ungrateful husband, and that monster of inconstancy did the like for an infamous mercenary strumpet, that would have licked the devil's cloven foot for half-a-crown. But nothing is so irregular as our appetites. A husband that has a pretty wife runs after a draggle tailed nasty servant wench. A nobleman that has his ragouts and ortolans, despises what he sees before him and calls for the sturdy beef and pottage that his footmen dine on. All the world has a depraved taste in many things, but your men of quality more than any. As they have more wealth than they know what to do with, and fondly perplex themselves in searching after what is never to be found, so they choose coarse ordinary things, only for variety's sake. Thus we see they spare neither pains nor money to purchase trifles ; and sometimes court some common jilt a twelvemonth before they can obtain those favours of her which she flings away upon others without asking. Heaven permits this, on purpose that they may punish themselves with an evil of their own seeking. Wretched man ! on whom Heaven has bestowed those two things that contribute to make life happy, riches in abundance, and a lovely wife. Riches to support and relieve those that deserve, but have them not, and to secure thee from stooping to those meannesses to which poverty often exposes the most generous souls ; and a wife that equals thee in quality, beautiful both in body and mind, wholly perfect in thy eyes, but much more so in those of others, who see farther into the affairs of their neighbour than their own ; and, in short, possessed of those shining qualifications, moderation, chastity, and virtue.

What is it thou art looking for elsewhere? Hast thou not at home thy other half, thy wife, whose wit can divert thee, who yields her body entirely to thy pleasure, who is jealous of thy honour, frugal of thy fortune, careful to preserve thy estate, who gives thee children to divert thee in their childhood, to support thee in thy old age, and to keep up thy name after thou art dead? What is it, I say, thou art looking after abroad? I will tell thee in few words, to ruin thy estate and reputation, to enfeeble thy body, to lose the esteem of thy friends, and, in a word, to create thyself abundance of enemies. Thinkest thou that thy honour is safe, because thou hast a virtuous wife? Alas! thou hast little experience of the things of this world, and art little acquainted with human frailty. The most tractable and quiet horse grows restive under an ill rider, and throws him to the ground. A woman may now and then resist a temptation to do ill, and yet commit a crime of much greater consequence, when she fancies herself most upon her guard. One fault draws many after it, and the distance between virtue and vice is sometimes not above a day or two's journey. And now methinks I see a malapert critic cock his hat, toss his wig over his shoulders, look fierce, and ask how these moral aphorisms come to be thus brought in hand over head. Why, pray, sir, don't be so choleric, make use of them or let them alone. as you shall see fit; 'tis all a case to your humble servant, I'll assure you; but under favour, sir, methinks you ought to thank the man who gives you them for nothing.

But to return to our story: Don Sancho was ready to rise from his young wife, when his uncle's steward brought him a letter, wherein the old gentleman sent him word of the strange lady who had visited him the night before, and whom he suspected to have cheated him, because she was not to be found in any of the inns in Toledo, whither he had sent to inquire after her. He desired him in the same letter to lend him one of his servants to pursue this notorious cheat to Madrid, whither he supposed she had steered her course, because he had sent his people upon all the great roads from Toledo to the neighbouring cities, and could hear no news of her. Don Sancho was not made of brass or marble. He found himself attacked in the weakest part of his soul, and was wondrous fierce and uppish to be once in his life wrongfully accused of a fault, who had been found guilty of so many before. The loss of so great a sum, and the sham that had been put upon his uncle equally incensed him. He told the story to his wife, and some of his relations, who came to give our new-married couple the good-morrow; and being not to be dissuaded from his resolution by the entreaty of his spouse, or the advice of his friends, dressed himself in a minute, ate a little breakfast, and ran to his uncle's house as hard as he could drive. The page, who had introduced Helen into the old marquis's chamber, described the coach to him, informed him how many they were in company, and by what marks they might be discovered. He took post from Toledo to Madrid, attended only by two footmen whose courage was not unknown to him. He rode four or five stages so fast, that he had no leisure to think of the beautiful stranger; but when his indignation was a little evaporated by his journey, Helen took place again in his fancy, so beautiful and charming was she in his imagination, that he was in the mind once or twice to return to Toledo to find her out. He wished himself a hundred times at the devil, for concerning himself so far about his uncle's robbery; and called himself sot, blockhead, and enemy to his own pleasure as often, to fatigue himself thus in riding post, whereas he might have employed his time to much better purpose, in seeking a happiness, the possession whereof, in his opinion, would have made him the happiest man in the world. While these amorous reflections took up his thoughts, he often talked to himself, as fools do, and that so loud, that his servants who rode before often stopped short, and turned back to inquire what he would have. "Why," would he often say to himself, "did I leave the place where I first beheld her, and shall not I be the most unhappy of men, if this stranger leaves Toledo before my return? Well, 'tis no more than what I deserve, who must needs take the office of a thief-catcher upon me unasked, unsought; but," continued he, "if I return to Toledo without doing anything, what will my friends say, who would have dissuaded me from this enterprise, and ought I to leave those villains unpunished that have robbed my uncle after so unheard of a manner, and besides, have so perfidiously wounded my reputation?" These different agitations employed the mind of our young extravagant, when near Xetaffe his footmen discovered Helen's coach by the tokens that had been given of it. They cried out with one voice to their master, "Yonder are the thieves," and without staying for him, rode up to the coach with their swords drawn. The coachman stopped, being terribly affrighted, and Montafar was much more than he. Helen ordered him to let down the glasses, and looked out to see how she could prevent so dangerous a storm. She saw Don Sancho riding towards her with sword in hand, whose angry countenance boded no good; but our amorous gentleman no sooner cast his eyes upon those two bewitching stars, which had so terribly wounded him, than his wounds bled afresh, and he immediately believed his servants had mistaken; for we have always a good opinion of the person we love; and as if he had known Helen from her cradle to have been a lady of unblemished virtue, laid about his footmen with his sword, like a distracted man. "You dogs," cried he, "you villains, did not I bid you have a care you did not mistake; and don't you deserve to have your throats cut for offering this rudeness to a lady who deserves respect from all mankind?"

The poor footmen, who had fallen so hastily upon the

coach, seeing it had all the marks the page had given them, and found within it a lady of so much beauty, which commands veneration even from the most brutal clowns kept off at a distance to avoid their master's fury, who thought he had reason on his side for what he had done, and that he was kind to them not to cut them to pieces. Don Sancho begged Helen's pardon, and acquainted her with the occasion why those sons of a thousand whores, his footmen, had attacked her so rudely, which she knew as well as himself. " See, I beseech you, madam," says he, " in what premunires these rascals may engage their masters; had not I happened to be with them, these blockheads upon a few foolish marks might have set the whole country in an uproar, raised the mob, and by mere force have carried you to Toledo for a thief. Not but that you are one," cries our gentleman, smoothing his countenance, " but, madam, you steal hearts, and nothing else."

Helen thanked Heaven within herself for giving her a face that stood her in such stead by clearing her from the wicked actions she used to commit, and recovering out of her fright, answered Don Sancho with a great deal of modesty, and in few words, knowing that to take a world of pains to clear one's self of a thing that is laid to one's charge, rather increases than lessens the suspicion. Don Sancho was surprised to find that treasure by mere accident which he had so violently longed to see, and was such a fool as to think that Heaven favoured his passion, since it had hindered him from going back to Toledo, as had been in his thoughts, which had he done, he had missed this happiness. He asked Helen what her name was, and where she lived in Madrid, and, moreover, begged her to give him leave to wait on her, that he might by his actions confirm the services he offered her. Helen told him both false : adding, she should think herself very happy to be honoured with his visits. He offered to see her safe home, but she would by no means consent to it, representing that she was married, and that her husband was to meet her on the road, therefore whispered him in the ear, that she was afraid even of her domestics, but much more of her husband's jealous temper.

This small confidence she seemed to repose in him made Don Sancho believe she did not hate him. He took his leave of her, and being carried swifter by his hopes than his trusty steed (if I may be allowed so to express myself) made the best of his way to Madrid. He no sooner arrived there, but he enquired after Helen, and her habitation, by the marks she had given him. His footmen were foundered in looking after her, nay, he employed all his friends upon this occasion, but to no purpose. When Helen, Montafar, and the venerable Mendez came to Madrid, their first care was how to get out of it. They knew well enough it would be impossible for them to escape the Toledo cavalier, and that if they stayed to give him a more particular knowledge of their merits, they should find him as dangerous an enemy as they took him now to be their humble servant. Helen disposed of all her movables, and next day after her arrival bought pilgrims' habits for herself and companions. In this equipage they beat the hoof towards Burgos, where Mendez was born, and where she had a sister of her own profession still living. In the meantime, Don Sancho, having lost all hopes of meeting with Helen, returned to Toledo, but so confounded and ashamed, that he did not speak one word from his setting out of Madrid till he came to his own house. After he had saluted his wife, who gave him a thousand caresses, she showed him a letter from his brother, who lived in one of the finest cities in Spain, where he had very good preferment in the cathedral church, and was one of the richest clergymen in all the country, wherein he sent him word that he was at the point of death. He stayed but a night at Toledo, and next morning betimes took post, either to contribute to his brother's recovery, or in case he died, to take possession of his estate.

In the meantime Helen pursued her journey to Burgos, being as much dissatisfied with Montafar as she had formerly loved him. He had shown so little bravery when Don Sancho and his footmen stopped their coach, that she did not question but he was a rank coward. This rendered him so odious to her, that she could scarce endure the sight of him ; her thoughts were wholly employed how to deliver herself from this domestic tyrant, and she flattered herself with hopes that she should soon get out of his clutches. It was the venerable Mendez that first put it into her head, and fortified this pious resolution, with all the reasons her prudence could suggest. This industrious matron was vexed to the very heart to see a lazy, useless lubber command her, govern Helen, and enjoy all the fruit of their labour, while he did nothing to obtain it. She incessantly represented to Helen the unhappiness of her condition, which she compared to that of a slave's working in the mines, who enriches his master with the gold he digs out of the earth with incredible labour and hardship, and instead of being the better treated for it, is commonly rewarded only with drubs and bastinadoes. She continually preached to her that beauty was a blessing of a short duration, and that her looking-glass, which showed her nothing now but what was amiable, and never spoke but to her advantage, would in a short time present her with a sight that would by no means please her, and tell her most dismal news.

"Madam," says she to her, "a woman that has seen thirty, loses every sixth month one of her charms, and sees some new blemish or wrinkle rise up every day in judgment against her face and body. That wicked thing called Time makes young women old, and old women wrinkled. If a woman that has enriched herself at the expense of her chastity and reputation, is for all that despised by the world, notwithstanding her wealth and fortune, think how wretched and miserable she must needs be that joins poverty to infamy; and what reason has she to flatter herself that any one will relieve her in her misery? If with the money you have acquired by certain means not approved by all the world, you should free an honest fellow out of jail and marry him, you would do an act pleasing both to God and man, and the end of your life would make some sort of atonement for the beginning of it. But you on the contrary throw away yourself and all you have upon a rascal, who is as villainous as he is cowardly, and who makes it his sole ambition to fleece poor women, whom he only gains by his menaces, and keeps under by his tyranny; now, under the rose be it spoken, this is to squander away one's wealth, on purpose to make one's self the greatest wretch alive, and to take pains to further one's ruin."

By these and such like discourses the judicious Mendez, who knew much better how to talk than act, endeavoured to remove the heroic Montafar from the good affections of the virtuous Helen, who had no other reason almost for loving him, but that she had been so long used to his company. Besides she was a woman of too good sense not to approve those reasons in her own thoughts, which the old matron had laid before her. In short, they were not urged to no purpose. Helen received them in good part, and so much the more readily, in that Mendez's interest alone was not concerned in them; and because at that time Montafar was coming up to them, that they might enter Gaudar-rama in a body, the place where they intended to dine. They adjourned, to a more convenient opportunity, their thinking of ways and means how to give him the slip, and get rid of him. He seemed much disgusted all dinner time, and going to rise from table was seized with a great shivering, and afterwards a violent fever, which held him the rest of the day and all night, and which increasing upon him next morning, gave Helen and Mendez some hopes that this lucky distemper might assist their designs. Montafar finding himself so weak that he was hardly able to crawl, gave our ladies to understand that they must not stir out of Gaudarrama, but must send for a doctor whatever it cost, and take all imaginable care of him. He spoke this with as much haughtiness and authority as if he had talked to his slaves, and was master of their lives as well as their money. In the meantime the fever found a way to his pericranium, and brought him so low, that if he had not called now and then for drink, one would have sworn he had been as dead as a door-nail. The people of the inn wondered why they delayed so long to send for a confessor to him, when Helen and Mendez, who did not doubt but this fever would give him a lift into the other world, sitting on both sides the bed, Helen began the following discourse:

"If thou canst remember, my dear Montafar," said she, "after what manner thou hast always lived with me, to whom thou hast had all the obligations imaginable, and likewise with Mendez venerable for her age and virtue, thou mayest easily imagine we shall not much importune heaven to restore thee to thy health, but although I should desire it as heartily as I have just reason to wish thy death, yet the will of heaven must be done, and I ought to offer up with the utmost resignation what I once loved most. To deal frankly by thee," quoth she, "for this is not a time to dissemble, both of us began some time since to be so weary of thy tyranny, that our parting was unavoidable, and if Providence had not kindly visited thee with this sickness, which will soon, we doubt not, do thy business, for know to thy consolation that thou art riding full gallop to another world, we would have endeavoured at least to have settled in some place in Spain, where we should have had no more thought of thee than if thou hadst never had a being. In short, whatever foolish inclination thou mayest have to live, thou oughtest to be very well pleased with thy death, since heaven, for reasons unknown to men, affords thee a more honourable end than thou dost deserve, permitting a fever to do that for thee which either the hangman generally does for such villains, or fear for such mean-spirited rascals as thou art. But, my dear Montafar," proceeded she, " before we part for good and all, tell me sincerely once in thy life, didst thou ever think I was such an arrant fool as to stay here to watch thee a nights, give thee thy juleps, potions, cordials, and administer thy clysters to thee ? Don't suffer such vanities as these to come into thy noddle when thou art so near death ; for though it concerned not only thy health, but that of thy whole family, I would not stay here a quarter of an hour longer. Cause thyself therefore to be immediately carried to some hospital, and since thou hast always followed my advice, don't despise this I now give thee, and which is the last thou art like to have from me. I mean, my poor Montafar, don't send for a physician, for he will most assuredly forbid thee wine, and that alone, without the help of a fever, were enough to kill thee in four-and-twenty hours."

While Helen talked thus, the charitable Mendez every now and then felt Montafar's pulse, put her hand on his forehead, and finding her mistress had done speaking. she re-assumed the discourse.

" In truth, Signor Montafar, your head is as hot as a glass-house, and I am mightily afraid this distemper will carry you off without so much as giving you leave to reflect on your past life. Take therefore this chaplet," added she, " and run over your beads devoutly till your confessor comes. This will do full as well for the discharge of your conscience. But if we may believe the annalists of the hangman of Madrid, that have so often employed their pens to describe your gallant exploits, your excellency's exemplary life will not require much repentance ; besides, heaven will reckon to you without doubt the dolorous perambulation

you made in the principal streets of Seville in the sight of
so many people, and guarded by so many officers on horseback, that one would have taken you for the sheriff, but that
he always marches at the head, and you were content at the
time to march in the rear. And what may yet farther help to
wipe off your scores, is your notable life at sea, where for
six years together, you did abundance of things pleasing to
your maker, working much, eating little, and always in
action ; and what is more considerable, you were scarce
twenty years old, when to the great edification of the
neighbourhood you began that holy pilgrimage. Nor is
this all," says our ancient matron, " for it is not to be supposed, but that you will be amply rewarded in the other
world for the care you have taken in this, that the women
that lived with you should not be lazy and inactive, making
them maintain themselves, not only by the labour of their
hands, but the sweat of their whole bodies. After all, if
you die in your bed, it must be an inexpressible consolation
to you, in that you will thereby put a pleasant cheat upon
the judge of Murcia, who swore a great oath he would make
you die in your shoes, who expects to have the satisfaction
to see you cut capers in the air, and, in a word, who will be
ready to hang himself when he comes to hear you were so
malicious as to die in your bed, without the help of a third
man. But I lose time in talking to thee, not considering
'tis high time to begin our journey, which we so earnestly
desire. And therefore, old friend of mine," continued she,
" receive this embrace with as good a heart as I give it, for
I am of opinion we shall see one another no more."

As soon as she had concluded this comfortable speech
Mendez threw her arms about his neck, Helen did the
like, and so they went out of the chamber, and soon after
out of the inn. Montafar, who had been accustomed to
their raillery, and could upon occasion return them a
Rowland for their Oliver, thought they had said all this
merely to divert him, and had not the least suspicion when

he saw them quit the room, fancying to himself they were but gone down to make him some water-gruel or posset-drink. After this he fell into a slumber, and though he could not be properly said to be fast asleep, yet it held him so long, that our damsels were got a league of their way before he awaked. He asked the woman of the inn where they were, she told him they were gone, and had given her orders not to disturb him, because he had not slept a wink the night before. Montafar then began to believe the lasses had left him in good earnest. He cursed the inn-keeper and inn to the pit of hell, threatened even the ground they walked upon, and the sun that gave them light. He must needs rise to put on his clothes, but was so feeble, he had like to have broke his neck. The good-natured hostess endeavoured to excuse the two damsels, and backed what she said with such impertinent reasons, as set our sick man a raving like one distracted, when he called her all the vile names he could think of. He was so vexed, that he would not eat a morsel for four-and-twenty hours ; and this no-diet, joined with plenty of choler, had that good effect, that after he had recruited himself with a little water-gruel, he found himself lusty enough to pursue his fugitive slaves. They were got two days' journey before him ; but two hackney mules that were sending back to Burgos farthered his design, as much as they ruined that of our two pretended pilgrims. He overtook them within six or seven leagues of Burgos, they changed countenance as soon as they saw him, and excused themselves as well as they were able. Montafar did not seem to be in the least angry with them, so great was his joy to have them again in his clutches. He laughed as heartily as they did at this merry frolic of theirs, and acted his part so well, that they believed him in their thoughts to be a downright passive blockhead. He persuaded them they had lost their way to Burgos, therefore leading them among some rocks, where he very well knew nobody would

come to interrupt him, he put his hand to a bayonet, to
which they had always paid a world of respect, and told
them, like a merciless devil as he was, that they must
immediately deliver all their gold, silver, and jewels. At
first they believed their tears would have accommodated
the business. Helen threw her arms about his neck, and
wept most plentifully; but our cavalier was so haughty,
now he had them in his power, that he was deaf to all
their prayers and entreaties, and signified to them his last
will and pleasure, that they must surrender all in a quarter
of an hour, otherwise they knew what they must expect.
Thus our poor damsels were forced to sacrifice their purses
for their safety, and it was with the last regret they parted
with their money, which they loved so dearly. But
Montafar's revenge did not stop here, for he produced
certain things called cords, which he had purposely
provided; and binding each of them to a tree, just over
against one another, told them with a treacherous smile
that, knowing how remiss and negligent they had been in
doing penance for their sins, he was resolved to give them
holy discipline with his own hands, that they might
remember him in their prayers.

He executed his pious design with some broom-branches,
and after he had satisfied himself at the expense of their
backs, he sat himself down between these two meek-hearted
sufferers, and turning towards Helen, spoke to her as
follows: "My dear Helen," said he, "take not in ill part
what I have done, but consider my good intention, and
know that every one is bound in conscience to follow his
vocation. It is thine to be malicious; for alas, the world
is composed of bad as well as good, and it is mine to
punish the malicious. Whether I have acquitted myself
as I ought, thou knowest better than any one; and if I
have heartily chastised thee, be satisfied I as heartily love
thee. If my duty did not render me deaf to all pity, I
would not leave so virtuous and honourable a damsel

naked, tied to a tree, and exposed to the mercy of the next passenger. Thy illustrious birth, with which thou didst lately acquaint me, deserves another destiny ; but I know thou wilt at the same time own, that thou wouldst do the same that I have done, if thou wert in my place. What falls out most unlucky is, that being so public as thou art, thou wilt be soon known ; and then it is to be feared that our magistrates, out of a maxim of policy, will order this wicked tree, with which thou art as it were incorporated, to be burnt, together with the wicked fruit it produces ; but know, to thy great comfort, that if thy wicked actions put thee now in bodily fear, the time will come when it will be a pleasure to thee to relate them, and when among thy other laudable qualities, thou wilt possess that of being able to pass a long winter's night, and set folks asleep with the recital of thy famous exploits. But I should give the good Mendez just occasion to complain of my unkindness should I address my discourse any longer to thee, without taking notice of her—nay, I should be wanting in my duty to my neighbour, if I should not in charity give her some advice that may be useful to her in the present posture of her affairs. They are," continues he, and turning himself towards Mendez, "in a worse condition than you imagine, let me persuade you, therefore, to recommend yourself seriously to your Maker, once in your life at least, since your old foundered carcass will scarce be able to support the fatigue of this day ; and oh! that my prayers could as easily procure you a confessor, as it is certain you want one. Not but that your exemplary life may leave your conscience in repose ; you have been so public-spirited and charitable all your days, that instead of censuring and magnifying the faults of others, you have repaired those of a thousand young maidens ; and since you have taken such pains to study the darkest and most concealed sciences, ought you not to be commended for it ? It is true, the inquisition has no

great kindness for you upon this score, nay, and has given
you some public marks of its displeasure ; but you know
that's composed of wicked men, and that it is natural for
people of the same profession to hate one another.   This
is not all, for those gentlemen have a very ill opinion of
your salvation ; but although what they say should be true,
yet a little time will reconcile one to the worst of places,
that is, even to hell itself, where you may take it for
granted you will soon receive all imaginable marks of
civility from the inhabitants, having conversed and dealt
with them from your infancy.   I have one word more to
say to you, and then I have done.   I might have chastised
you, madam, after another manner, but I considered that
old people, according to the proverb, turn children again,
and your ladyship is old enough to be in your first state
of innocence, and therefore whipping was more proper for
the little trick of youth you played me, than any other
chastisement.   And thus, ladies, I take my leave of
you, earnestly desiring you to have a care of your dear
persons."

Having rallied them after this fashion, justly or not, as
the reader pleases, away he went, and left them rather
dead than alive, not so much for grief of their having been
whipped, as because all their money was gone, and they
were left in a lonely place tied to trees, where they might
expect every minute to be devoured by wolves.   With
these melancholy contemplations in their pates, as they
were looking sorrowfully upon one another, without saying
a word, a hare crossed the road before them, and some
time after a greyhound thundering after poor puss, and a
cavalier well mounted thundering after the greyhound.
Who should this now be but Don Sancho de Villafagnan,
who had made a journey to Burgos to see his sick brother,
and kept him company at a country house not far from
thence, whither he had retired to take the fresh air.   He
was extremely surprised to behold two women thus bound

to their good behaviour, but much more, when he found one of them to resemble the beautiful stranger whom he had seen at Toledo, whom he sought after at Madrid, and whom he had ever since perpetually in his mind. Being firmly persuaded she was a woman of quality and married, he doubted whether this was she, for he could not imagine what should bring her into that part of the world in so wretched an equipage. But Helen's face having lost nothing of its former lustre, though somewhat disordered by her fright, made him to conclude that he at last had accidentally met with that treasure which had cost him so many desires and inquietudes in the pursuit of. So he raised himself in his stirrups to see whether the coast was clear, and was fool enough to suspect that this was nothing but a diabolical illusion, which Heaven had permitted to punish him for his sensuality. Helen on her part was taken up with a thought full as mortifying, for she fancied her ill stars had chosen this unlucky day to show her to all that had anything to say to her. Don Sancho looked upon her with great amazement, and she on him with no less disorder ; each expected when the other should speak, and Don Sancho at last was going to begin, when a servant came full speed to tell him that some of his relations were going to kill one another. Upon this he spurred his beast, attended by the servant ; and when he came to the place where he left his company, he found some four or five drunken fellows, calling one another rogue and rascal, with their tilters in their hands, and flourishing them notably in the air, to the prejudice of some neighbouring trees, that lost some of their best branches by the bargain. Don Sancho, though enraged to be deprived of the charming vision he had so lately seen, did nevertheless all he could to reconcile these furious, terrible gentlemen ; but all his arguments, entreaties, and menaces had signified nothing, had not the wine that over-loaded their brains, and down-right lassitude tripped up their heels, and left them snoring

on the ground, as peaceably as if they had never fallen
out. Don Sancho seeing this, spurred his horse back
towards the happy tree, which kept the idol of his heart,
and was at his wits' ends when he saw the women were
gone. He turned his eyes round him, to see which way
they could be escaped, but saw nothing but a lonely,
melancholy place; he spurred his horse afresh, and
examined every corner, and at last came back to his
beloved oak, which like a good natured tree as it was, still
kept its old station. But as Don Sancho was a poet, and,
what is more, a tender-hearted whining poet, he had not
the same indifference for this insensible tree as other men
have. He alighted from his horse, and harangued it after
the following manner, or at least should have done so, if
he were really so great a coxcomb as I have been told
he was:

"O thrice happy trunk! since thou hast had the
honour to be embraced by that divine creature, whom I
love without knowing her, and whom I know only because
I love her, may thy leaves ever shine among the stars: let
the sacrilegious axe never presume to wound thy tender
bark; may the thunder reverence thy boughs, and the
worms of the earth not dare to approach thy root; let the
winter spare, and the spring adorn thee; let the proudest
pines envy thy condition; and lastly, may Heaven protect
thee in every part." While our worthy gentleman was
spending himself in these vain contemplations, or, if you
please, these poetical follies, which, by the by, are of
greater importance than others are, and ought not to be
used every day in the week, his servants, who knew not
what was become of him, after they had looked for him a
pretty while, at last found him and brought him home.
He returned to his brother's house very much concerned at
his late adventure; and unless I am mightily mistaken, I
have heard some people say, he went supperless to bed.
Some critics now will perhaps tell me I have left my

reader too long in suspense, who without question is impatient to know by what strange enchantment Helen and Mendez came to disappear to the amorous Don Sancho. But let him have patience, and I will soon inform him.

Montafar was at first pleased with that piece of justice he had done upon the two fugitives ; yet no sooner did the heat of his revenge begin to cool, but love inflamed him, and represented Helen to his thoughts infinitely more charming than he had ever fancied her before. He considered within himself that the prize he had taken from her would be soon spent, whereas her beauty was a certain revenue to him, so long as he kept in with her, whose absence was already become insupportable to him. So he came back the same way he went, and with those individual barbarous hands, that had so rigorously bound the two dames to the trees, and afterwards so unmercifully lashed them, broke their chains, that is to say, either cut or untied their cords, for historians differ, and by that means set them at liberty, at the same time that Don Sancho was employed not far off to reconcile his drunken companions, who were in a very fair way to cut one another's throats. Montafar, Helen, and Mendez shook hands upon this reconcilement, and after they had mutually promised to forget all was past, embraced with as much tenderness as if nothing had happened ; doing just as your great people do, who neither hate nor love, but accommodate these two contrary passions to their interest, and the present state of their affairs. They deliberated which road to take ; and it was agreed *nemine contradicente*, that it was by no means advisable for them to go to Burgos, where they would be in danger of having their quarters beaten up by the Toledo cavalier. Therefore they pitched upon Seville for the place of their retreat, and fortune seemed to favour their designs ; for coming into the Madrid road, they met a muleteer with

three empty mules, who agreed to carry them to Seville
at the very first proposal Montafar made him. He took
care to regale our damsels on the road, to make them
forget the ill treatment they had received from his hands.
At first they could hardly bring themselves to trust him,
and had resolved to be revenged on him the first opportunity that presented ; but at last, rather for reasons of
state than any principle of charity, they became better
friends than ever. They considered that discord had
ruined the greatest empires, and believed they were in all
probability born for one another. They did not think fit
to give any specimen of their profession upon the road to
Seville, for as their design by shifting their country was
only to get at a distance from those that might pursue
them, so they were afraid of bringing themselves into new
trouble, which might hinder their getting to Seville where
they had great designs to put in execution. They alighted
within a league of the city, and having satisfied the
muleteer, got thither about the dusk of the evening, and
took up their lodgings at the first inn they found. Montafar
hired a house, furnished it with very ordinary furniture,
and dressed himself all in black, with a cassock, and a long
cloak of the same colour. Helen took upon her the habit
of a religious sister, that had devoted herself to works of
piety ; and Mendez went dressed like a saint, valuing
herself upon her hoary locks, and a huge monstrous
chaplet, each bead of which was big enough to load a
demi-culverin.

The very next day after their arrival Montafar showed
himself in the streets, apparelled as I have already described him, marching with his arms across, and looking on
the ground whenever he met any women. He cried out
with a shrill voice, that was enough to have rent a rock,
" Blessed be the holy Sacrament of the altar, and the thrice
happy conception of the immaculate Virgin ! " and uttered
many more devout exclamations, with the same everlasting

lungs of leather. He made the children whom he met in the streets repeat the same words after him ; and moreover assembled them sometimes together, to teach them to sing hymns and songs of devotion, and to instruct them in their catechism. He repaired to the gaols, and preached to the prisoners, comforting some and relieving others, begging victuals and other provisions for them, and frequently walking thither with a heavy basket upon his back.

O detestable villain! thou wantedst nothing but to set up for a hypocrite to be the most profligate accomplished rascal in the universe. These actions of virtue, in a fellow that was the least virtuous of all mankind, procured him in a little time the reputation of a saint. Helen and Mendez likewise did all that in them lay to deserve canonization. The one called herself the mother, the other the sister of the thrice blessed friar Martin. They went every day to the hospitals, where they assisted the sick, made their beds, washed their linen, and did all this at their own expense. By these means the most vicious people in Spain obtained the universal admiration of all Seville. About this time a gentleman of Madrid happened to come thither about some private affairs. He had formerly been one of Helen's lovers, for women of her character have commonly more than one string to their bow. He knew Mendez to be a notorious cheat and Montafar to be no better. One day as they came out of the church, encompassed by a great number of persons, who kissed their very garments, and conjured them to remember them in their prayers, they were known by the aforesaid gentleman, who, burning with a Christian zeal, and not able to suffer three such notorious impostors to abuse the credulity of a whole city, broke through the crowd, and giving a hearty box o' th' ear to Montafar,

"You wicked cheats," cried he, "do you neither fear God nor man ? " He would have said more, but his good intention, which in truth was somewhat of the rashest, had not the success it deserved. All the people fell on him, whom

they believed to have committed sacrilege in offering this
violence to their saint.   He was beaten to the ground, and
had certainly been torn to pieces by the mob, had not
Montafar by a wonderful presence of mind undertaken his
protection, by covering him with his body, keeping off
those that were most enraged against him, and exposing
himself even to their blows.

"My brethren," cried he to them as loud as he could
bawl, "let the poor wretch alone for the love of God ; be
quiet for the love of the Blessed Virgin."   These few words
having appeased this horrible tempest, the people made
room for Brother Martin to pass, who went up to the
unfortunate gentleman, well pleased in his heart to see him
so used, though showing outwardly a mighty concern for
him.   He raised him up from the ground, embraced and
kissed him all covered as he was with blood and dirt, and
reprimanded the people for their rude behavour.

"I am a wicked man," said he to the standers by, "I am
a sinner, I am one that never did anything pleasing in the
eyes of God.   Do you believe," continued he, "because you
see me dressed in this religious garb, that I have not been
a robber all my lifetime, the scandal of others, and the
destruction of myself?   Alas! you are mistaken, my
brethren. Make me the mark of your contumelies, pelt me
with stones, nay, draw your swords upon me!"   Having
spoken these words with a counterfeit sorrow, he threw
himself with a zeal yet more counterfeit at the feet of his
enemy, and kissing them, not only begged his pardon, but
likewise gathered up his sword, cloak, and hat, which he
had lost in the scuffle.   He helped him on with them
again, and leading him by the hand to the end of the
street, took his leave of him, after he had bestowed
abundance of embraces, and as many benedictions on him.
The poor man was as it were out of his wits at what he
had seen, and with what had been done him, and was so
full of confusion, that he durst hardly show his head in the

streets all the while his affairs detained him at Seville.
Montafar had won the hearts of all the city by this
pretended act of devotion. The people gazed at him with
admiration, and the children cried after him, " A saint, a
saint," as they cried out, " A fox, a fox," when they saw his
enemy in the street. From this moment he lived the
happiest life in the world. Some nobleman, cavalier,
magistrate, or prelate perpetually invited him to dinner,
and strove who should have most of his company. If he
were asked his name, he would answer, he was a beast of
burthen, a sink of filth, vessel of all iniquity, and such like
noble attributes, which his counterfeit devotion dictated to
him. When he visited any of the ladies, he complained to
them incessantly of the nothingness of his dispensation,
and the deadness of the inward man : adding, he wanted
concentration of heart, and recollection of spirit ; in short,
he always talked to them in this magnificent cant and
holy gibberish. No alms were given in Seville but what
passed through his hands, or those of Helen and Mendez,
who were not wanting likewise to act their parts to
admiration, and stood as fair for a red-lettered preferment
in the almanack, I mean to be sainted, as Montafar
himself. A lady of quality, who was a widow, and devout
even to superstition, sent them every day two dishes of
meat for dinner, and as many for supper, and you must
know these dishes were dressed by the very best cook in
all Seville. Their house was too little to receive the
numerous presents were daily sent them. A woman that
had a mind to be with child put her petition into their
hands, to the end, by their mediation it might be presented
to the tribunal of heaven. Another that had a son in the
Indies did the same, as likewise a third that had a brother
prisoner in Algiers. Nay, the poor widow who had to
contest with a powerful adversary before an ignorant or a
covetous judge, did not doubt the success of her cause
when she had once made a present to them according to

her ability. Some gave them sweetmeats and conserves, others pictures and ornaments for their closet. Several charitable persons trusted them with great quantities of linen and woollen cloth, to dispose among the needy that were ashamed to beg, and with considerable sums of money to distribute as they saw convenient. No one came to visit them empty-handed, and their future canonization was as firmly believed as an article of faith. At last the credulity of the people ran so high, that they came to consult them about their doubtful affairs, and things to come.

Helen, who was as subtle as a devil, managed all the answers, delivering her oracles in few words, and those capable of receiving different interpretations. Their beds were mean and homely, covered in the daytime with coarse blankets, but at night with all the fine furniture a man could desire, that loves to sleep deliciously ; their house being plentifully furnished with good feather-beds, fine coverlids, and, in short, with all sorts of movables that contribute to the convenience and pleasure of life : and all this they pretended was to be given to some poor widow, whose goods had been seized in execution, or to furnish some young woman's house who had married without any fortune. Their doors were shut up in winter at five, and in summer at seven o'clock, as punctually as in a well-regulated convent ; and then the jack was wound up, the spits turned merrily round, the capons put down to the fire, the table handsomely spread, when our hypocritical triumvirate ate heartily, and drank plentifully to their own, and the healths of those people they had cheated. Montafar and Helen lay together for fear of spirits, and their footman and maid, that were of the same complexion, copied so pious an example. As for the good Mendez, she always lay alone, being more taken up with contemplation than action, ever since she had addicted herself to the black art. This was their constant practice. instead of employing their time in mental prayer, or in doing penance. 'Tis no wonder if, living so jolly a life, they looked plump and fat. All the city blessed heaven for it, and were mightily surprised that persons of so much austerity and self-denial should look better than those that lived in luxury and ease.

For the space of three years they deceived the eyes of all the inhabitants of Seville, and by receiving presents from every one, and appropriating to their own use the alms that passed through their hands, they had heaped together an incredible number of pistoles. All good success was ascribed to the efficacy of their prayers ; they stood god-fathers to all children, made matches for all the city, and were the common arbitrators of differences. At last heaven was weary of conniving longer at their impious lives. Montafar, who was choleric in his temper, used frequently to beat his valet, who could not bear it, and had quitted his service a hundred times if Helen, who was more discreet than her gallant, had not prevented it by appeasing him with fair words and presents. One day having drubbed him immoderately for little or no reason, the boy got to the door, and, blinded by his passion, ran directly to the magistrates, to inform against these three hypocrites whom the world took for saints. Helen's diabolical spirit foretold what would happen, therefore advised Montafar to rub off with all the gold they had in the house, and retire to some place of security, till this tempest, which threatened them, had spent itself. It was no sooner said than put in execution. They carried off the most valuable things, and walking down the street as unconcerned as if they had dreaded nothing, went out at one gate, and came in at another, on purpose to baulk the scent of their pursuers. Montafar had insinuated himself into the good graces of a widow, as vicious and rank a hypocrite as himself. He had communicated this secret to Helen, who was no more jealous of this matron than Montafar would have been of a gallant

that would have promoted the good of their little common-
wealth.   Here they absconded in safety, and lived luxuri-
ously, the widow loving Montafar for his own sake, and
Helen for Montafar's.   In the meantime the justice was
conducted by the vindictive valet to the famed mansion
of our pretended saints.   When he came there he found the
birds flown, and the maid not able to inform him whither
they were gone.   However, he sealed up all their trunks,
and took an exact inventory of all that was in the house.
The serjeants found more provision in their kitchen than
would have served to regale them one day, and you may be
sure they took care to lose nothing that they could privately
sink to their own use.

In the midst of this bustle the venerable Mendez entered
the house, little imagining what had happened.   The
serjeants apprehended her, and carried her to prison with
a vast concourse of people at her heels.   The servant and
maids were likewise sent thither to bear her company, and
having talked too much, as well as the old matron, were
condemned, as well as she, to receive two hundred lashes.
Mendez died three days after this chastisement, it being
somewhat of the severest for a person of her age, and the
servant and maid were banished Seville for their lives.
Thus the foreseeing Helen preserved her dearly beloved
Montafar and herself from the hands of the magistrates,
who searched after them in vain, both within and without
the city.   The people were all ashamed to be so notoriously
cheated ; and the ballad singers, who had sung their praises
the week before, now employed their hackney sonneteers
to expose these pretended saints in lamentable doggerel.
These insects of Parnassus exhausted all their little stock of
scandal upon this subject, and the wretched rhymes they
composed against these godly cheats, who, not long before
were the idols of the people, are still sung in Seville.

Montafar and Helen took the road to Madrid as soon as
they could do so with safety, and arrived there rich, and in

the circumstances of husband and wife. The first thing they did was to enquire after Don Sancho de Villafagnan, and finding he was not in Madrid, appeared in public ; he dressed as fine as a lord, and she in the equipage of a woman of quality, and as beautiful as an angel. She was married to Montafar, as has been said before ; but it was upon this condition, that like a husband of good sense and great patience, he should not take ill the visits her beauty occasioned her ; and she on the other hand obliged herself to receive none but such as would turn to their common advantage.

Your goers between, otherwise styled promoters of good intelligence between the two sexes, vulgarly called bawds, or, to speak more honourably of them, women of intrigue, soon came acquainted with Helen, and directed her how to manage herself. One day they made her show herself at the play, next day in the park, and sometimes in the high street of Madrid in her coach, where, bestowing a glance upon one, a smile upon another, and giving hopes to all, she soon furnished herself with a set of lovers enough to man a galley. Her dear husband religiously observed every article of the original contract ; he encouraged his wife's bashful gallants by his obliging behaviour, and led them as it were by the hand to her apartment, where he was so courteous and discreet, that he always pretended some extraordinary business or other called him out, in order to leave them by themselves. He scorned the acquaintance of any that were not rich and would not spend their money freely, and never knocked at the door till he was assured by a certain signal that always hung out of his window when his virtuous spouse was taken up in private business, that his presence would spoil no sport ; and if the aforesaid signal forbid his coming in, he trooped off merry and well satisfied, as knowing business went on in his absence, and passed away an hour or so at some gaming academy, where every one caressed him for his wits' sake.

Among the rest that paid tribute to Helen, a certain

gentleman of Granada surpassed all his competitors in his excess of love and expenses. He was descended of so good a family, that the titles of his nobility were to be found in the archives of the capital city of Judea, and those that were particularly acquainted with his pedigree have affirmed, that his ancestors were the hangmen of Jerusalem, both before and after Caiaphas. His great affection for Helen made him release a great number of pistoles out of an obscure dungeon, where he had imprisoned them for many years. In a short time Helen's house became the best furnished of any in Madrid. A coach and four that cost her nothing the keeping, came punctually every morning to receive her orders, and waited on her whither she pleased to command them till night. This prodigal lover took one of the side boxes at the play-house for her for a whole twelvemonth, and scarce a day passed over his head, but he provided some magnificent collation or other for her and her friends, at one of the summer houses near Madrid. Montafar, who loved his belly like to any churchman, never failed to make one of the number. He went as fine as a prince, had as much money in his pocket as a clerk of the treasury, ate like a Frenchman, and drank like a German. He paid a wonderful deference to our Granada gentleman who was so very liberal of his money, and indeed he had naturally an esteem for persons of that character. But at last the wind veered about, and raised a terrible storm. Helen now and then used to receive visits from a young swaggering spark, one of those furious heroes that never made a campaign in their lives, yet talk of nothing but slashing and killing, that live upon some wretched harlot, whom they insult at discretion, that go every day to the play-house to pick pockets, or create quarrels, and who at night draw their swords and hack against some passive wall, swearing next morning they had been engaged in a dangerous encounter the night before with at least half a dozen bullies. The sage Montafar often told Helen he was not at all pleased to see such a visitant in his house, from whom they could expect nothing. But for all he could say to her, she was not in the mind to part with her gallant. Montafar was angry with her, and to make himself some amends out of her carcass, treated her with the same chastisement which Mendez of happy memory and she had formerly undergone in the mountains of Burgos. Helen pretended to be easily reconciled, however meditated secret revenge in her heart. The better to accomplish her end, she caressed him so lovingly for eight days together, that he persuaded himself she was one of those tractable ladies that adore their tyrants, and use their humble servants scurvily.

One day that our Granada gallant had promised to sup with them, but by reason of some unexpected business could not come to the noble entertainment he had provided for them, Montafar and Helen drank hand to fist several bumpers to their benefactor, to whom they were obliged for all this good cheer. Montafar got fuddled according to his laudable custom, and towards the end of the repast must needs taste a bottle of perfumed hippocrass, which the gentleman had sent them as an extraordinary present. It is not certainly known whether Helen, who opened the bottle before supper, put any poisonous drugs in it or not: but this is agreed on all hands, that soon after Montafar had emptied it, he felt a strange heat in his bowels, and intolerable pains after that. He suspected he was poisoned, and ran towards his sword, at the same time that Helen did the like towards the door, to avoid his fury. Montafar went into his chamber, thinking she had hid herself there, lifting up the tapestry, but discovered Helen's young gallant, who without any more ceremony whipped him through the guts. Montafar, though he had received his death's wound, yet held him fast by the throat. The servants made such a hellish noise with crying out murder, that the justice coming that way ran into the house, just as the young bravo, who had done Montafar's business, was making his escape. In the meantime Helen, who had got into the street, and knew not which way to take, ran into the first house she found open. She saw a light in a lower room, and a cavalier walking up and down in it. Without asking him any questions, she threw herself at his feet to implore his assistance and protection, and was strangely surprised to find it was Don Sancho de Villa-fagnan, who on his part was no less astonished to see the idol of his heart thus prostrate, this being the fourth time of his meeting her by accident. Don Sancho had lately fallen out with his wife, who had procured herself to be divorced from him, upon the score of his ill usage of her, and his disorderly life. He had obtained a commission to go and settle a new colony in the Indies, and was to embark at Seville in a short time. Helen told him a thousand lies ; and he was ravished to find she was ready to follow him into America: the justice apprehended the assassin of Montafar, and made a strict search after Helen in Madrid, and seized all they could find in her house. Don Sancho and Helen arrived happily in the Indies, where several adventures befell them that cannot be contained in so short a volume as this is, and which I promise to oblige the public with, under the name of the *Perfect Courtezan, or the Modern Lais,* if I find the world inclined to receive it.

NOVEL IV.

THE INNOCENT ADULTERY.

THE Spanish court at Valladolid was very much bedaggled and bemired, where they are as much bedaggled as
they are at Paris, according to the observation of a famous
Spanish poet, when in one of the coldest raw nights of a
very cold raw winter, and about the time when most of our
convents ring to matins, a young gentleman, Don Garcias
by name, came out of a house where he had spent the
evening in conversation, or else play. He was now got
into the street where he lodged, and although the night
was exceeding dark, by reason the sky was overcast, yet
had he no light with him, whether it was because his footman had lost his link, or because he was a gentleman that
did not stand upon these punctilios, I cannot tell; when a
door opening all on the sudden, he saw somebody thrown
out of it with that violence as to fall on the other side the
way. If he was surprised at so odd an adventure, he was
much more so when, going to lend his hand to this person
that had been so rudely treated, he perceived she was in
her smock, and heard her sigh and lament, without making
the least effort to rise. He concluded she might be hurt
with the fall, therefore by the help of his footman having
set her on her legs again, he desired to know wherein he
might serve her.

" 'Tis in your power to save both my life and honour,"
answered this unknown person in a voice interrupted with
frequent sobs, and which discovered she was a woman.
" I conjure you," added she, " by the same generosity that
inclined you to pity my misfortunes, to carry me to some
place of security, provided none but yourself, or such whose
fidelity you can trust, may know where I am."

Don Garcias covered her with his cloak, and commanding his footman to bear her up on one side, as he did on
the other, soon arrived at his lodging, where everybody was
gone to bed but the maid, who opened the door, and cursed
them heartily for making her sit up so late. All the
answer the footman made her was blowing out the candle,
which while she went to light, calling him a hundred rogues
for his pains, Don Garcias conducted, or rather carried the
afflicted lady, who could scarce make a shift to stand, to
his room, which was up one pair of stairs. His man soon
brought a light, and then Don Garcias beheld one of the
most beautiful women in Spain, who at the same time in-
spired him with both love and compassion. Her hair was
as bright and black as jet, her complexion a mixture of
lilies and roses, her eyes two suns, her breasts above all
comparison, her arms admirable, her hands much more so,
and her shape like that of a queen, of one's own creating :
but this black hair was in disorder, this charming complexion was eclipsed, these piercing eyes were top full of
tears, these incomparable breasts were bloody, these arms
and hands were in no better condition, in short, this fine
body so delicately shaped was covered all over with black
and blue marks, as if it had undergone the discipline of a
dog-whip a cat-of-nine-tails, or something as bad.

If Don Garcias was ravished to behold so beautiful a
creature, this beautiful creature was as much concerned
to see herself in her present circumstances, in the power of
an unknown gentleman, who seemed not to be above
twenty-five years of age. He was sensible of it, and did

all that in him lay to persuade her she had no reason to
fear any ill usage from a man who should think himself
happy to die in her service.   In the meantime his footman
made a little coal-fire, for in Spain they use scarce any
other firing, which by the by is none of the best in the
world.   He laid a pair of clean sheets, or at least he ought
to have laid them, on his master's bed, who wishing the
lady a good night, left her in possession of his chamber,
which he double locked, and went to lie, upon what pretence
I cannot imagine, because our history is silent in the matter,
with a gentleman, an acquaintance of his, that lodged in the
same house.   He slept in all probability much better than
his guest, who wept all night long.   The day appeared,
Don Garcias arose, and dressed himself as spruce as a
courtier for a ball.   He listened at his chamber door, and
hearing the poor lady still bemoaning herself, made no
difficulty to come in.   As soon as she saw him, her grief
attacked her with new violence.

" You see," says she to him, " a woman who was yesterday the most esteemed in Valladolid, now infamous to the
last degree, and that deserves more to be pitied than ever
she did to be envied ; but let my misfortunes be never so
great, the charitable protection you have so seasonably
afforded me may still alleviate them in some measure, if
at night you will see me conducted in a chair or coach to a
certain convent I shall name to you.   But," continued she,
" after so many obligations ought I to beg the favour of
you to step to my house, and inform yourself what is said
and done there ; and, in short, to know after what manner
the court and city talks of an unfortunate woman, whom
you have so generously protected ? "

Don Garcias offered to go wherever she would please to
command him, with all the eagerness of a man who begins
to be in love.   She gave him all the instructions that were
necessary upon this occasion : he took his leave of her, promising to return immediately, when she, poor lady, fell a

weeping and lamenting as violently as if she had begun but that very moment. Don Garcias did not stay a full hour before he came back, and finding his beautiful guest as much afflicted as if she already knew that he had ill news to impart to her,

"Madam," says he to her, "if you are Eugenia, the wife of Don Sancho, I have something to tell you which nearly concerns you. Eugenia is not to be found, Don Sancho is in the hands of the magistrate, accused of the murder of his brother Don Lewis."

"Sancho is innocent," cries she ; "I am the unfortunate Eugenia, and Don Lewis was the most wicked of all men." Her tears which trickled down apace, and her sighs which redoubled their violence, would not give her leave to say any more ; and in all probability Don Garcias was not a little perplexed to put on a sorrowful air to keep her company in her grief. At last, as violent things are never of long continuance, Eugenia's affliction began to abate, she wiped off her tears, her sighs were gentler than before, when she reassumed her discourse in the following manner :

" 'Tis not enough that you know the name and quality of the unhappy woman you have so highly obliged, she is likewise willing to acquaint you with the particulars of her life, and to testify in some manner her gratitude to you by reposing this confidence in you. I am," continued she, " descended from one of the best families in Valladolid. I was born rich, and with beauty enough to give me some pretence to be proud of it. The charms of my person brought me more lovers than those of my fortune, and the reputation of both together provided me adorers in the remotest parts of Spain. Among the rest who believed they should be happy in possessing me, Don Sancho, and Don Lewis, two brothers, equally befriended by fortune and nature, signalized themselves by the excess of their passion, and the mutual emulation there was between them, who should render me the most important services. My relations declared themselves in favour of Don Sancho, who was the eldest, and my inclination following their choice, I gave up myself entirely to a man of above forty years old, who, by the sweetness of his temper, and the extraordinary care he took to please me, had made as great a progress in my affections, as was possible for any person whose age had been no better suited to mine. The two brothers, notwithstanding they were rivals, had all along lived very amicably together, and Don Sancho when he had married me did not lose the friendship of his brother Don Lewis by so doing. Their houses were contiguous, or, properly speaking, were but one house ; for the wall that divided them had a door, which by common consent was always left open. Don Lewis did not forbear to pay the same *dévoirs* to me before his brother as he had done while he was his rival, and Don Sancho, whose love increased after possession, and who loved me better than his life, was not in the least offended at his gallantry. He himself was used to call me his brother's mistress, who on his side made a real love to pass for a feigned one, with so much address, that I was not the only person he deceived by it. In short, after he had accustomed me to hear him talk of his passion before company, he made love to me in private with so much importunity, and so little respect, that I no longer doubted his intentions were criminal. As young as I was, I had discretion enough to make him still think I took his love to be only meant in raillery. I made a jest of what he spoke in earnest, and though I was never more enraged than at that time, yet I laboured as well as I could not to lose my ordinary temper. He was provoked at it, instead of making right use of it, and looking upon me with eyes, which his wicked designs had made wild and staring: ' No, no, madam,' says he, ' I feign much less since I have lost you, than I did when I had some hopes to possess you ; and though your rigour be sufficient to deliver you soon from the importunities of your lover, yet have you so long accus-

tomed me to suffer, that you will do much better to———'
'Never to be alone with you if I can help it,'said I interrupting him.

"One of my women that came into my room at that
time, hindered him from carrying his insolence farther, and
me from showing him my resentment as he deserved, and I
was about to do.   I was afterwards very glad I did not do
it, as well for my husband's sake, as because I was in
hopes this wicked brother of his would at last love me less,
and come to esteem me more ; but still he continued to make
feigned love before company, and to solicit me in private.   I
combated his transports with all the severity I could sum-
mon to my aid ; nay, so far as to threaten him to acquaint
his brother with it.   I used all my arts to cure him of this
folly.   I prayed, I wept, I promised to love him as much
as any brother ought, but he forsooth would be loved as a
lover.   In short, sometimes a sufferer, sometimes ill-treated,
but always as much in love as he was hated, he had made
me the most unhappy woman in Spain, if my conscience,
that can reproach me with nothing, had not preserved
tranquillity to my soul.   But at last my virtue, which had
all along so well defended itself against so dangerous an
enemy, abandoned me, because I abandoned it first, and
helped to betray myself.   The court came to Valladolid,
and brought all its gallantry along with it.   As all new
things are apt to please, our ladies fancied they saw more
in the courtiers than they could find in the city gallants,
and the courtiers endeavoured to please our ladies, whom
perhaps they looked upon as assured conquests.   Among
the other cavaliers that attended the court, in hopes of
being recompensed for their services, a Portuguese, whose
name was Andrada, had rendered himself one of the most
considerable by his wit and good mien, but much more by
his expensive way of living, the most efficacious charm to
gain women of no experience, who judge of the beauty of
the soul by that of the equipage or habits.   He had no

great fortune of his own, but play had made him master of that of other people, and his gains this way were so considerable, that he made as great a figure as the richest and most magnificent nobleman at court. I was unfortunate enough to please him, and when my own vanity, backed by his continual addresses, had persuaded me I was not disagreeable to him, I reckoned myself the happiest woman upon earth. I can hardly express how well he knew how to make himself beloved, or to what excess I loved him. My husband, so good, so dear, and so respected, became to me in a little time as contemptible as odious, Don Lewis appeared more hateful to me than ever. In short, nothing pleased me but Andrada. I loved none but him, and in all places where I did not see him, I surprised all the company with my distractions and restless behaviour. Andrada on his part loved me full as passionately. His predominant passion for gaming gave way to his love; his presents gained my women; his letters and verses charmed me, and his serenades set all the husbands in our street a thinking for whom they were designed. In short, he attacked me so well, or I defended myself so ill, that I at last surrendered. I promised him all that lay in my power to give him, so that now we had no other difficulty to surmount, but that of a convenient time and place.

" My husband had engaged in a hunting-match, which would keep him several days in the country. I sent to acquaint my dear Portuguese with this news, and we agreed to execute our amorous designs that very night, after my husband was gone. I was at a certain hour to leave the back door of our garden open, and under pretence of passing part of the night there, by reason of the excessive heats, was to set up a field-bed in a little summer-house, that was open on all sides, and encompassed with orange trees and jessamines. At last my husband quitted Valladolid, and that day seemed to me the longest I ever knew. The night came, and my women having set me up

a bed in the garden, I pretended to be very sleepy, and as
soon as my maids had undressed me, commanded them all
to go to bed except one chamber-maid, who knew the secret
of our amour : I had scarce laid me down, and the maid,
whose name was Marina, had hardly shut the garden-door
that faced the house, and opened the back-door, when
my women came to tell me my husband was returned.   I
had but just time to shut the garden-door, which I had
ordered to be left open for Andrada.   My husband caressed
me as he used to do, and you may imagine how I received
him.   He told me he was forced to come back, because the
gentleman who had invited him to the sport had unluckily
fallen off his horse, and broke his leg.   After this he commended my judgment for choosing so cool and refreshing
a place, and concluded he would likewise take up his
quarters there.   He got himself undressed at the same
time, and came to bed to me.   I did all I could to conceal
my vexation at his return, and to show him by my feigned
embraces that his were not ungrateful to me.   In the meantime Andrada came at the hour of assignation, and finding
the door shut, which he thought to have found open, by the
help of his valet leapt over the garden-wall, where he had
hoped to pass the night with me.   He has confessed to me
since, his jealousy put him upon so hardy and dangerous a
design ; and that he did not doubt but some happy and
better beloved rival enjoyed that happiness which I had
promised him.   These suspicions of his, that perhaps I
diverted myself at his expense with another gallant, so inflamed his anger, that he was resolved to use me ill, in case
he found what he suspected to be true, and to revenge himself upon his rival to the last extremity.   He crept up to
the summer-house, whereby we lay together, as softly as he
could.   The moon shone very bright, I saw him, and knew
him as soon as he came in ; he saw I was very much
affrighted, and I made a sign to him to be gone.   At first
he could not discern whether the person that was in bed

with me was my husband or some one else ; but observing in my countenance less fear than confusion and shame, and seeing upon the table the clothes and plume of feathers he had seen my husband wear that very day, and which were as singular as they were remarkable, he was satisfied it was Don Sancho whom he saw a bed with me, and found him to be faster asleep than a gallant in all probability would have been. However, he drew near that part of the bed where I lay, and stole a kiss, which I could not well hinder, considering the fear I was in lest my husband should awake. He had no mind to keep me longer in this fright, and therefore went his way, lifting up his eyes to heaven, shrugging his shoulders, and showing all the marks of a man that was deeply afflicted at this disappointment, and so leapt back again over the garden wall with the same facility as before.

" Early in the morning I received the most passionate letter from him that ever was read, accompanied with a pretty copy of verses upon the tyranny of husbands. He spent the remainder of the night, after he had parted with me, in writing them, and next day when I received them, I could hardly do anything else but read them over and over, as oft as I could do it in private. Neither of us sufficiently reflected upon the hazard we had run to make it a warning to us not to expose ourselves so any more. But although I had not been inclined of myself to grant him all he asked of me, or had loved Andrada less than I did, or had not yielded to the insinuating flattery of his letters, yet I could not have resisted the persuasion of my chamber-maid, who talked to me incessantly in his favour. She reproached me with want of resolution, which had made me to think no more of Andrada, and talked of the passion he had for me with the same vehemence as she would have told a sweetheart of her own what a kindness she had for him. By this I found she was not to learn her trade now, and likewise saw of what importance it is to be careful in the choice of persons that are placed so near women of my age and condition.

But I was resolved to ruin myself, so that if she had been more virtuous than she was, she had enjoyed a less share in my confidence.   At last she over-persuaded me to receive Andrada in a dressing-room near my chamber, where she lay by herself; and we agreed that so soon as my husband was fast asleep she should lie by him in my place, while I passed the night with my gallant.   Thus we got him concealed into my dressing-room ; my husband fell asleep, and I prepared to meet my lover with all the emotions of one whose desires are violent, yet who had a great deal to fear, when a terrible noise of confused voices that cried out 'Fire, fire,' alarmed my ears, and waked my husband.   At the same time my chamber was all in a smoke, and I could perceive the flames through my windows.   A negro maid, that served in the kitchen, had set it on fire, being drunk, and it was not perceived till it had taken hold of some dry wood, and the neighbouring stables, and now had seized my apartment.   My husband was very well beloved.   In an instant the house was full of neighbours that came to help us to quench the fire.   My brother-in-law Don Lewis, whom the common danger had made more active and diligent than the rest, was one of the first that helped us with his servants, and who, pushed on by his passion, soon made his way into my chamber through the flames, that had already seized the staircase.   He was in his shirt, and had nothing over it but his night-gown, in which he wrapped me up, when taking me between his arms, who might more properly be said to be dead than living, and that on account of the danger to which Andrada was exposed, rather than my own ; he carried me to his own room, through the communication his house had with ours, and setting me down upon his bed, left me there, accompanied by some of my women.

"In the meantime my husband, and all that had concerned themselves in this accident that had befallen us, bestirred themselves so notably, that the fire was happily

put out, yet after it had done a great deal of damage.
Andrada made his escape without difficulty among the
crowd and press of people that came to help us ; and you
may imagine how joyful I was when Marina told me the
agreeable news.   He writ to me a hundred foolish things
the next day, which I answered with more transport than
he had shown ; and thus we made shift by writing to each
other to soften and relieve that pain which absence occasioned us.   After we had repaired all the mischief the fire
had done us, and I had left Don Lewis's room to return to
my own, Andrada easily persuaded me to let him try the
same way once more, which had not failed the last time but
for so unfortunate and unexpected an accident.   That very
night we had pitched upon to make ourselves full amends
for the time the fire had made us to lose ; a cavalier of my
husband's acquaintance, who was in some trouble about a
duel, and had fled to an ambassador's house, where he did
not think himself safe enough from the civil magistrate,
was obliged to abscond somewhere else.   My husband
carried him privately to his own house, and took the key of
the street door, which he caused to be locked before his
face, lest any servant through treachery or indiscretion
might discover the place of his retirement.   This order, at
which I was equally surprised and troubled, was unluckily
put in execution just as Andrada made the signal in the
street, which he had told Marina of before.   The poor
maid was in a strange quandary what to do, and made him
a sign from a low lattice window to stay a moment.   We deliberated upon the matter a little, and afterwards she went
and told him in a low voice what new obstacle our ill-
natured destiny had trumped up to oppose our design ; so
she proposed to him to stay till all our people were gone
to bed, and then he should try to get in through one of the
kitchen windows, which she would open to him.

"Nothing seemed difficult or dangerous to Andrada, provided he could but satisfy his love.   My husband saw his

friend to bed, and went to bed himself in good time, after the example I had set him ; all our servants did the like ; and Marina, when she thought the whole family was fast asleep, opened the little window to Andrada, who with all the ease in the world got half way through, but so indiscreetly or unfortunately, that after several efforts, which rather did him a mischief than helped him, he stuck fast by the waist between the iron bars, without being able to stir backwards or forwards. His valet could not help him from the street, no more could Marina from the place where she was, without some one else to assist her. So she went to call up one of the maids, in whom she could repose confidence, and told her that she had been over-persuaded that night by her sweetheart, whom she loved entirely, and was to marry in a little time, to try to let him in at the kitchen window, but that he stuck so fast between the iron bars, that there was no getting him out without filing, or wrenching them out of their places ; she desired her therefore to assist her in this extremity, to which the other readily consented ; but for want of a hammer, or some such like iron utensil, Andrada had not been a farthing the better for the help of these two wenches if he had not bethought himself of his poignard, which did the business so effectually, that after a great deal of struggling and sweating, the iron bars were by main strength wrested from the wall, and my gentleman delivered from the terrible fear of being found so scandalously wedged, in a place where he could be taken for nothing but a house-breaker. However this could not be done with so little noise but that some of the servants heard it, who looked into the street, at the same time when Andrada, carrying with him the iron hoop, which enclosed him about the waist, ran off as hard as he could drive, attended by his footman. The neighbours and our servants cried out 'Stop thief' after them, and made no question but that some villains had attempted to rob Don Sancho's house, especially when they saw the iron bar, gone. In the meantime Andrada got safe to his lodgings, and was forced to file off the iron bar, which gripped him as close as a belt, for notwithstanding all the tricks his man and he played, there was no getting it off otherwise.

" This third accident put him in a very ill humour, as I came to be informed afterwards. As for me, I took it quite otherwise ; and while Marina, not yet recovered of her fright, told me the story, I thought I should have killed myself with laughing. However, I was no less concerned than he at this series of disappointments, which rather inflamed than cooled our desires, and would not let us defer the happy minute of enjoyment any longer, than the very next day after this pleasant but unlucky adventure. My husband was in the city, endeavouring to make up his friend's business for him, which in all probability would keep him there the remaining part of the day. I sent trusty Marina to Andrada's lodgings, that were not far from my house, she found him a bed still discomposed with the fatigues of the last night, and so dejected by these unlucky crosses in his amours, that Marina was partly scandalized to see with what coldness he received the advances I made him, and to find him so backward to give me the meeting, although she often assured him this was an opportunity that was not to be lost. To make short of my story, at last he came, and I received him with all the transports of joy which a woman wholly abandoned to her passion can feel. I was so blinded by it, that I did not perceive, as well as Marina did, with what indifference he made his approaches to me, although it was but too visible. However my embraces at last drew on his. Hitherto our mutual joy could not be otherwise expressed than by our silence, and the thoughts of what each of us desired with so much ardour put me into so great a confusion, that I could not look Andrada in the face, and by this means gave him an opportunity to attempt what he pleased ; when Marina,

who like a discreet chamber-maid had gone out of the
room to be upon the watch, came in all affrighted and
told me my husband was come home.   She carried
Andrada into my dressing-room, rather dead than alive,
and seeming to be much more concerned than myself,
although I had more reason to be so.   My husband gave
some orders to his people below, before he came up into
my chamber.   In this interval I had just time enough to
compose myself, and Marina to empty a great coffer full
of lumber, into which she put the despairing Andrada.
She had scarce stowed my lover in this little sanctuary,
when my husband came into the room, and only kissing
me as he passed by, without any farther stay, went directly
into my dressing-room, where he found a book of plays
and unhappily opened it.   He lighted upon a place that
pleased him, and had engaged him to read longer, if
Marina had not advised me to go to him, and try to bring
him into my chamber.   My misfortunes did not stop here,
for Don Sancho, finding me strangely discomposed and
thoughtful, as I had but too much reason to be, endeavoured by his own good humour to put me into a
better.   Never in his life did he take so much pains to
divert and please me as now, and yet never did he vex and
importune me more.   I begged him to quit my chamber,
pretending to be so sleepy that I could not hold open my
eyes ; but by an unseasonable fit of pleasantry, which was
not usual with him neither, he kept me company in spite
of all I could say to him ; and though he was the most
complaisant man alive, yet showed he so little of it at this
time, that I was forced to turn him out.   As soon as ever
I had locked my chamber door, I ran into my dressing-
room to deliver Andrada from his prison.   Marina opened
in all haste the coffer wherein she had put him ; but both
of us had like to have died of fear and grief, when we
found him without either pulse or motion like a dead man,
and so in effect he was according to all appearance.

" Imagine to yourself what terrible agonies this sight occasioned me, and what measures it was possible for me to take in so cruel an extremity. I wept, tore my hair, grew desperate, and I believe had had resolution enough to have stabbed myself with Andrada's poniard, if my excessive grief had not so enfeebled me, that I was forced to throw myself upon Marina's bed. This maid, although she was concerned to the last degree, yet preserved her judgment better than I in this our common calamity, and bethought herself how to remedy it ; which for my part I wanted strength to execute, although my reason had not been disordered after the manner it was. She told me that perhaps Andrada was only in a swoon, and that a chirurgeon either by bleeding, or some other speedy relief, might restore him that life which he seemed to have lost. I looked on her without returning any answer, my grief having in a manner made me stupid. Marina lost no time in asking more questions, but went immediately to put in execution what she had proposed ; but no sooner had she opened the door with this intention, than my brother-in-law Don Lewis popped in upon us, and this second disaster was yet more terrible than the first. Although the body of Andrada had not been exposed to his view as it was, yet the confusion and surprise he might read in our faces would have told him that we had been engaged in some mysterious affair, which he would not have failed to examine to the bottom, being so much interested in me, both as a brother-in-law and a lover. I was therefore obliged to throw myself at the feet of a man whom I had often beheld at mine, and, relying upon the love he had for me, and upon his generosity, the essential quality of every gentleman, resigned the dearest thing I had in the world entirely to his will. He did what he could to raise me, but being resolved to continue on my knees, I frankly told him, as well as my tears and sighs would give me leave, what a sad accident had befallen me, at which I don't at all question but he was pleased in his heart. ' Don Lewis,' said I to him, ' I don't implore thy generosity now to prolong my life ; my misfortunes already have made it so odious to me, that I would even take it away myself, were I not afraid that my despair could not effect it, but at the expense of my honour, from which that of Don Sancho, and even his life, are perhaps inseparable. Thou mayst believe the disdain I have all along shown thee was rather the effect of my aversion than virtue ; thou mayst rejoice at my disgrace, nay, and glut thy revenge with it ; but darest thou reproach me with a crime which thou hast so often tempted me to commit, and canst thou want indulgence for her who has so often shown it to thee ? ' Don Lewis would not let me go on, but, ' Madam,' says he, ' you see heaven has justly punished you for bestowing your affections upon one whom you ought to have hated : but I have no time to lose, that I may convince you by drawing you out of this premunire, that you have not a better friend in the world than Don Lewis.'

"Having said this, he left me, and returned a moment after with two porters, whom he had ordered to be sent for. Marina and I had, in the meantime, put Andrada's body again into the great coffer. Don Lewis lent a helping hand to put it on the fellows' shoulders and bid them carry it to a certain friend's house of his, to whom he had discovered this adventure, as he had before entrusted him with the secret of his amour. Here, after he had taken the body out of the coffer, he ordered it to be laid at full length on a table, and while they were taking off his clothes he felt his pulse, and put his hand on that part of his breast where the palpitation of the heart is best to be discovered, whereby he found there were still some sparks of life remaining in him. He sent for a chirurgeon in all haste, while in the meantime they put him to bed and employed all the remedies proper to bring him to life again. In short, he came to himself, being blooded. A servant was left to attend him, and the company quitted the room to afford time to nature and rest to complete that cure which their remedies had so successfully begun. You may imagine how great Andrada's surprise was when, after so long a *deliquium*, he found himself in bed, and could only remember what a fright he had been in when they put him into the coffer ; he knew not where he was, nor what he had to hope or fear. He was taken up with these mortifying thoughts, when he heard the chamber-door open, and when the curtains were drawn saw by the light of some tapers that were brought into the room, Don Lewis, whom he very well knew to be my brother-in-law, and who, having taken a chair, spoke to him as follows : 'Am I a stranger to you, Signor Andrada, and don't you know I am brother to Don Sancho ?' 'Yes,' replied Andrada, 'I know you well enough.' 'And do you remember,' cries Don Lewis, 'what happened to you to-day at his house ? Take my word for it,' continues he, 'if you pretend any more to carry on your intrigues with my sister-in-law, or if I ever see you more in our street, you shall sorely repent it ; and further know, that thou hadst been a dead man if I had not taken compassion on a foolish and unfortunate woman, who has been pleased to put her life and honour into my hands ; and if I were not fully assured that thy criminal designs against my brother's honour have not been put in execution. Change your habitation therefore,' continues he, 'and think not to escape my resentments if you break the promise I expect you should make me.' Andrada promised him more than he asked, he made him the meanest and most abject submissions he could think of, and protested that he owed him a life for saving his. He was weak enough in all conscience to keep his bed, but his excessive fear gave him strength to get up. From that very moment he conceived as great an aversion for me as his affection before had been violent, nay, he had my very name in horror. In the meantime I was uneasy to know what was become of him, but had not assurance to ask Don Lewis, nay, not so much as to look him in the face. I sent Marina to Andrada's lodgings, where she arrived just at the same time as he came in himself, and had ordered his trunks to be got ready, to remove to another quarter of the town. As soon as he saw her, he forbade her to come to him any more from me ; and recounting in few words all that had passed between Don Lewis and himself, added that I was the most ungrateful and most perfidious woman in the world ; that he would only consider me for the future as one that designed to ruin him, and desired I would no more think of him than if I had never seen him. Having said this, he turned Marina out of his chamber, who was extremely surprised at his treatment. However her astonishment was not so great but that she had presence of mind enough to dog him at a distance, and observing the house where his trunks were carried, by that means came to know his new lodgings.

"The vexation I felt to be accused of a crime whereof I was innocent, and to be hated by the man whom I loved so tenderly, for whom I had hazarded both my life and reputation, hindered me from taking so much satisfaction in his safety as otherwise I should have done. I fell into a fit of melancholy, which threw me into a sickness, and my distemper, which the physicians could not tell what to make of, was no little affliction to my husband. To complete my misfortune, Don Lewis began to value himself upon the important service he had done me ; he incessantly importuned me to grant him that happiness which I had intended for Andrada : reproaching me that I was in love with the latter, all the time I preached to him what I owed to my husband, and what he owed to a brother. Thus, being hated by the man I loved, loved by him I hated, seeing Andrada no more, seeing Don Lewis too often, and perpetually accusing myself for having been so ungrateful to the best husband in the world, who left nothing undone to please me, and who was distracted at my

illness, when he had the justest provocations to take away
my life ; being thus troubled with remorse of conscience,
of love and hatred, two passions so contrary, I kept my
bed for two months, expecting every moment my death
with joy ; but heaven, it seems, reserved me for greater
misfortunes. My youth, in spite of myself, assisted me
against this inconsolable grief. In short, I recovered, and
Don Lewis persecuted me much more than ever he had
done. I had given orders to my women, and particularly
to Marina, never to leave me alone with him. Enraged at
this usage, and the resistance I continually made him, he
resolved to obtain by the blackest piece of treachery that
ever was known that which I refused him with so much
steadfastness. I have already told you there was a way
from his house to ours, through a door that was seldom
shut. On the night he pitched upon for the execution of
his damnable design, and at the hour when he thought
every one was asleep, both at his house and ours, he got in
by this door, opened the gate towards the street, and
turned all our horses out of the stable. They immediately
ran into the court, and thence into the street. The noise
they made soon awakened the servants that looked after
them, and they my husband.

" He being very fond of his horses, as soon as ever he
knew they were got into the street, immediately ran after
them in his morning gown, swearing heartily at his
grooms, and the porter, who had forgot to shut the great
gate. Don Lewis, who had hid himself in my ante-
chamber, and seen my husband go down stairs, followed
him into the court, and having shut the street door, and
tarried a little to give the greater probability to what he
had a mind to effect, came to bed to me, personating my
husband so well, that 'tis no wonder if I was mistaken.
He was excessive cold with standing so long in his shirt.
' Good God, sir,' said I to him, ' how cold you are.' ' 'Tis very
true,' answered he, counterfeiting his voice, ' I had like to

have been starved in the street.' 'And are your horses,' said I to him, 'retaken?' 'My servants are gone after them,' cries he; and then drawing nearer me, as to warm himself, embracing me very lovingly, proceeded to betray me, and dishonour his brother. As heaven permitted this crime, perhaps it reserved the punishment of it to me, that so my honour might be retrieved by my own hands, and my innocence known. Having satisfied his wicked desire, he pretended to be in pain for his horses, so up he got, and having opened the street gate, retired to his own lodging, well pleased perhaps with his crime, and rejoicing in that which would be the cause of his destruction. My husband came in soon after, and getting into bed crept close to me, half frozen and starved as he was, and obliged me by his caresses, which I thought extraordinary, to desire him to let me sleep. He thought it strange; for my part I was surprised, and did not doubt but that some treacherous trick had been played me. I could not sleep a wink till it was day, I got up much earlier than I used to do, went to mass, and there I saw Don Lewis in his finest clothes, and with his countenance gay, as mine was sad and melancholy. He presented me with the holy water, which I received very coldly from him; then looking on me with a malicious sneer, 'Good God, madam,' says he, 'how cold you are!' At these words, that were the same I spoke to him the night before, and which made me no longer doubt my misfortune, I turned pale and then reddened. He might easily find by my eyes, and the disorder he had occasioned me, how heinously I resented his insolence. I parted from him, without so much as looking at him, and passed all the time at mass very uneasily, as you may well imagine. I made my husband uneasy too, when at dinner, and all the rest of the day, I looked like a distracted woman, sighing incessantly, and showing that I was troubled in mind, notwithstanding all the care I took to conceal it. I retired to my chamber sooner than I used to do, pretending a slight indisposition. I thought of a hundred different designs to revenge myself.

"At last my indignation put me upon that which I resolved to put in execution. The night came, I went to bed when my husband did. I pretended to sleep, to oblige him to do the same ; and when I saw him fast, and supposed all our servants were so too, I got up, took his poniard, and, wholly blinded and transported by my passion, made a shift however by the same door, and the same way through which my cruel enemy had got to my bed, to find the way to his. My fury made me not to do things at random. I groped out where his heart lay with my hand that was free, and discovered it by its palpitation. My fear of missing my blow did not make the other tremble wherein I held the poniard. I sheathed it twice in the heart of the detestable Don Lewis, and punished him by a gentler death than he deserved. In the heat of my rage I gave him five or six hearty stabs more, and returned to my chamber in that tranquillity and peace of mind that convinced me I had done nothing but what was just. I put up my husband's poniard, bloody as it was, into the scabbard. I dressed myself in as much haste, and with as little noise as I could ; I took with me all my jewels and money, and as much transported by my love as I had been lately hurried by my revenge, ran away from my husband, who loved me better than his life, to throw myself into the arms of a young man who had not long ago taken care to let me know I was become odious to him. The natural cowardice of my sex was so well fortified by the impetuous passions that reigned in my soul, that though it was midnight, and I all alone, yet I walked from my own house to Andrada's lodging, with as much assurance as if I had being going to do a good action in the daytime. I knocked at Andrada's door, who was not at home, being engaged, it seems, at play at a friend's house. His footmen, who knew me well enough, and were not a little surprised to see me there, received me with a great deal of respect, and lighted a fire for me in their master's chamber. He came home soon after, and I suppose little imagined to find me in his room. He no sooner saw me, but looking wildly upon me, cried, 'What has brought you hither, Madam Eugenia, and what have you to say to me, of all men living, whom you designed to sacrifice to the revenge of your brother-in-law and gallant?' 'How! Andrada,' said I to him, 'do you put so ill a construction upon an unavoidable accident, which forced me to have recourse to the only man in the world whom I was most afraid to be obliged by? and could you pass so disadvantageous a judgment on a person who had given you so many proofs of her affection? I expected something more than reproaches from you, which you would not have been in a condition now to make, had I not done that very thing for which you condemn me, and charge me with as a crime. Alas! if I had been guilty of any, it is not against you, but against my husband, to whom I ought to have been faithful, to whom I have been ungrateful, because I would not be so to you, and whom I have left to cast myself upon a cruel man that uses me ill. When your death, which I looked upon to be real, had flung me into that despair, which how could a woman avoid, that expected every moment to be surprised by her husband? and when Don Lewis found me in this deplorable condition, what could I otherwise do than rely upon his generosity, and the love he had for me? He has most treacherously betrayed me at the expense of his own honour, but it has been also at the expense of his own life, which I have just now taken from him; and 'tis this, my dear Andrada, that has brought me hither. It is necessary I should conceal myself from justice, till I find a proper time to inform the world what Don Lewis's crime was, as well as my own misfortune. I have money and jewels enough to maintain you with splendour in any part of

Spain, whither you will think fit to accompany a miserable woman. I shall convince the whole world in a little time that I rather deserve to be pitied than blamed, and my future conduct shall justify my past actions.' 'Yes, yes,' cried he, interrupting me, 'I will go and take Don Lewis's place, now thou art cloyed with him, and have my throat cut like him, when thou art so with me.' Ha! thou lascivious woman,' continues he, 'how well does this last wicked action of thine confirm me in my belief that thou designedest to sacrifice me to thy gallant? but think not to come off with reproaches only, I will rather be the punisher of thy crime than the accomplice of it.' He had no sooner spoke these words, but he stripped me by main force, in so barbarous a manner, that even his servants were ashamed of it; he gave me a hundred blows, naked as I was, and after he had satisfied his rage till he was quite weary, threw me into the street, where, if I had not happily met with you, I had died ere this, or fallen into the hands of those who perhaps are now searching for me."

When she had ended her discourse, she showed Don Garcias the black and blue marks on her arms, and those parts of her body which modesty would allow her to show, and then resumed as follows:

"You have heard, generous Don Garcias, my deplorable history: tell me, therefore, I conjure you, what measures an unhappy woman ought to take, who has caused so many calamitous misfortunes."

"Ah, madam," cries Don Garcias interrupting her, "that I could as easily advise you what to do, as punish Andrada, if you would but give me leave! Don't rob me of the honour of revenging your quarrel, and don't refuse to employ, in whatever you think fit to command, a man who is no less concerned for your misfortune, than the outrage which has been offered you."

Don Garcias pronounced these words with a heat which convinced Eugenia he no less loved than pitied her. She thanked him in the most obliging terms her civility and gratitude could suggest, and begged him to give himself the trouble to go once more to her husband's house, to inform himself more particularly what people said of her flight, and of the death of Don Lewis. He happened to come there just at the time they were carrying Don Sancho to prison, together with his domestics, and those of Don Lewis, who had deposed their master was in love with Eugenia. The common door between the two houses which had been found open, and the poniard of Don Sancho yet reeking with blood, were circumstantial proofs that he had murdered his brother, of which nevertheless he was as innocent as he was afflicted at it. The running away of his wife, his jewels and money that were missing, so strangely surprised him, that he could not tell what to make on't, and this troubled him infinitely more than his imprisonment and the proceedings of the magistrate. Don Garcias was impatient to carry this news to Eugenia, but could not do it so soon as he desired. One of his friends, who had business with him, stopped him a long while in the street where his lodging was, that happened to be over against Andrada's, from whence he saw a servant come out booted, carrying a portmanteau. He followed him at a distance, accompanied by his friend, and saw him stop at the post-house. He came in after him, and found he had hired three horses, that were to be got ready in half an hour. Don Garcias let him go, and ordered the same number of horses to be ready at the same time. His friend asked him what was the meaning of this, he promised to tell him, provided he would make one of the number ; to which the other readily consented, without troubling himself what the matter was. Don Garcias desired him to put on his boots, and stay for him at his lodgings, while he made a short trip to his own. Thus they parted ; and Don Garcias went immediately to wait upon Eugenia to inform her what he knew of her affair. At the same time he gave orders to his landlady who was a woman he could trust, to furnish Eugenia with clothes and other necessaries, and to carry her that very night to a convent, the abbess whereof was her relation and friend. After this he privately ordered his man to carry his riding coat and boots to the gentleman's lodgings whom he last parted with, and having once more conjured the woman of the house to take care of Eugenia, and conceal her from all the world, he went to call upon his friend, and walked with him to the post-house, where they had not been a minute but Andrada came thither. Don Garcias asked him whither he was going. He told him to Seville.

"Why, then," replied Don Garcias, "we shall need but one postilion." Andrada liked the notion, and perhaps thought Don Garcias and his friend were a brace of cullies, whom he might easily bubble of their money at play. They rode out of Valladolid together and galloped a pretty while, without doing anything else ; for I think 'tis agreed on all hands, that when men ride post, they are none of the best conversation. Don Garcias, finding they were now in a fine open plain, fit for business, and remote enough from any house, rode a little way before the company, then came back and bid Andrada stop. Andrada asked him what he would have. "I must fight you," answered Don Garcias, "to revenge, if I can, Eugenia's quarrel, whom you have mortally injured by the most cowardly and villainous action that ever was known."

"I don't repent of what I have done," replied Andrada to him fiercely, without seeming to be surprised, "but perhaps you may have occasion to repent of this insolence." He was a man of courage, and alighted from his horse at the same time that Don Garcias alighted from his, who would not vouchsafe him an answer. They were now coming up to one another with their swords drawn, when Don Garcias's friend told them they must not offer to tilt without him, and offered to fight Andrada's footman, who was a well-shaped young fellow, and of a promising countenance. Andrada protested, that although he had the best swordsman in all Spain for his second, he would only fight one against one. His footman, not contenting himself with his master's protestation, protested likewise, for his part, that he would fight no man whatever, for what cause whatever, or at any weapon whatever. So Don Garcias's friend was forced to be an humble spectator, or, if you please, godfather to the two combatants, which is no new thing in Spain. The duel did not last long, heaven so much favoured the righteous cause of Don Garcias, that his enemy, pressing upon him with more fury than skill, ran upon his sword's point, and fell down dead at his feet, losing his blood and life together. Andrada's footman and the post-boy, neither of whom were made for heroes, threw themselves at the feet of Don Garcias, who meant them no mischief. He commanded Andrada's footman to open his master's portmanteau, and give him all he had taken from Eugenia. He obeyed him immediately, and put into his hand a rich manteau, gown, and petticoat, and a little box, which by its weight would have made a blind man swear it was not empty. The footman found the key of it in his master's pocket, and gave it likewise to Don Garcias, who bid him do what he pleased with his master's body, threatening to cut his throat if he ever saw him in Valladolid. He commanded the post-boy not to come back till the dusk of the evening, and promised he should find the two horses he had hired at the post-house. I suppose he was punctually obeyed by these two worthy gentlemen, who were ready to die with fear, and thought they were exceedingly obliged to him, for not killing them as he had done Andrada. History leaves us in the dark as to what his footman did with his body ; and as for his movables, it is very probable he kept them for his own use. Our memoirs likewise are wanting to inform us how the post-boy managed himself in this affair. Don Garcias and his friend galloped it all the way to Valladolid, and alighted at the imperial ambassador's house, where they had friends, and stayed till it was night. Don Garcias sent for his footman, who told him Eugenia was in pain to see him. The horses were sent back to the post-house by an unknown person, who cunningly ran off after he had delivered them to one of the ostlers. As for Andrada's death, the people of Valladolid either talked nothing at all of it, because they never heard a word of it ; or if they talked anything of it, they said no more but that a cavalier had been killed by some unknown enemy, or by thieves.

Don Garcias returned to his lodgings, where he found Eugenia dressed in the clothes which his landlady had taken care to provide for her. I am apt to believe she took them up at a broker's ; for in Spain it is a common thing for persons of quality, both men and women, to rig themselves in such places. He restored Eugenia her things again, particularly her jewels, and informed her after what manner he had revenged her quarrel upon Andrada. Being of a sweet and tender disposition, she was extremely concerned at the unfortunate end of a person whom she had once so dearly loved, and the thoughts that she was the cause of so many tragical disasters, afflicting her as much as her own misfortunes, caused her to shed abundance of tears. That day public notice had been given at Valladolid that no one should entertain or conceal Eugenia, and two hundred crowns were offered by way of reward to any that could bring any news of her. This made her resolve to get into a convent as soon as she could. However she passed that night in the lodging where she was, and slept as little as she did the night before. Don Garcias rose by break of day to go visit the abbess of the convent, who was related to Eugenia, and promised to receive, and keep her private, as long as she was able. From thence he went to hire a coach, and ordered it to stop at a by-street adjoining to

his, whither Eugenia came, accompanied by the gentlewoman of the house, both of them covered with their veils.
The coach carried them to a certain place, where they
ordered the coachman to set them down, and there
alighted that no one should find out the convent whither
Eugenia had retired. She was courteously entertained
there ; Don Garcias's landlady took leave of her, and went
to inform herself how matters were like to go with Don
Sancho. She was told things looked with an ill aspect,
and that the least they talked of doing to him was putting
him to the question. Don Garcias communicated this
news to Eugenia, who was so much concerned to see her
husband in danger of being punished for a crime he was no
ways guilty of, that she was resolved to surrender herself
into the hands of justice. Don Garcias dissuaded her from
so doing, and advised her rather to write to the judge-
criminal to let him know that only she could inform him
who it was that killed Don Lewis. Upon this the judge,
who by good luck was related to her, went attended with
several other officers of justice to discourse her. She
freely confessed to them that she had killed Don Lewis,
acquainted them with the just provocation he had given
her to serve him so, and recounted to them the particulars
of all that had passed between Don Lewis and herself,
except what related to Andrada. Her confession was
taken down in writing, and a report of it made to his
catholic majesty, who, considering the blackness of Don
Lewis's crime, the just resentment of Eugenia, her courage
and resolution, the innocence of Don Sancho and his
domestics, ordered them all to be set at liberty, and
granted his royal pardon to Eugenia, at the instance of all
the court, who appeared in her behalf. Her husband was
not much displeased with her for the death of his brother,
nay, if one knew the truth, perhaps loved her the better for
it. He made her a visit as soon as he was enlarged, and
would fain have taken her home with him, but she would

not consent to it, notwithstanding all his importunities and entreaties. She did not question but that he took Don Lewis's death as he ought to take it, yet knew very well he had heard something of what had passed between her and the Portuguese cavalier ; and that the least blemish in a woman's honour may raise her husband's jealousy, and sooner or later untie the conjugal knot, let it be never so well knit. Poor Don Sancho visited her often, and endeavoured by all the tenderest instances of kindness he could show her, to oblige her to return home, and be absolute mistress of his estate and him. She continued inflexible in her resolution, reserving for herself a pension suitable to her quality and fortune.

But though Don Sancho could not prevail on her to go home with him, yet she behaved herself so obligingly to this good husband, that he had all the reason in the world to speak well of her. But all that she did in the convent to please him only increased his concern that he was not able to get her out of it. This threw him at last into so deep a melancholy, that he fell sick, and his sickness brought him to death's door. He conjured Eugenia to afford him the satisfaction of seeing her, before he parted with her for ever. She could not refuse this sorrowful delight to a husband who had been so dear to her, who had loved her so tenderly, and who still loved her so well. She went to see him die, and had like to have died herself with grief, to observe him show so much joy at the sight of her, as if she had restored that life to him which he was going to lose. This goodness of Eugenia did not go unrewarded. He left her all he had, by which means she became one of the richest and beautifullest widows in all Spain, after she had found herself upon the very brink of being one of the most unhappy women in the world, Her affliction for the death of her husband was sincere as it was great. She gave all necessary orders for his funeral, took possession of his estate, and returned to her convent, resolving to pass the remainder of her days there. Her relations proposed to her the best matches in Spain, but she was resolved not to sacrifice her repose to her ambition ; and finding herself everlastingly persecuted by crowds of pretenders, whom her beauty and wealth drew after her to the parlour of the convent where she was, she would at last be seen by nobody but Don Garcias. This young gentleman had served her so opportunely upon so important an occasion, and with so much zeal, that she could not see him without saying to herself that she owed him something more than bare civilities and compliments. She discovered by his livery and equipage that he was not over rich, and she was generous enough to offer him some assistances, which a person in ordinary circumstances may receive without shame from one that is richer than himself. In the little time she had been at his lodgings, and in the conversation he had often had with her, he made her sensible he had a lofty soul, elevated above the common pitch, entirely disengaged from all sordid interests, and wholly devoted to honour. She was therefore afraid she should affront him if she made him any present, which to be sure would have been answerable to her generous temper ; and on the other hand she feared he would have but a sorry opinion of her gratitude, if she did not give him some proofs of it by her liberality. But if Don Garcias gave her some pain upon the aforesaid occasion, she gave him no less on her part, and so was even with him. In short, he was in love with her, but though the respect he bore her could not have hindered him from acquainting her with it, yet how durst he mention love to a woman, whom that word had so lately exposed to such terrible misfortunes, and that at a time, too, when the sorrowful air of her face, and the tears which trickled down her cheeks incessantly, were evident demonstrations that her soul was yet too full of grief to be capable of admitting any other passion.

Among the rest that made their visits to Eugenia, in

quality of her thrice humble slaves, in hopes I suppose to become one day her thrice imperious masters ; among the rest, I say, who had offered themselves to her, and whom she had refused, there was one Don Diego, who having nothing else to distinguish him, was resolved to signalize himself by his constant persecutions. He was foolish as it is possible for a young fellow to be, as unmannerly as he was foolish, as troublesome as he was unmannerly, and hated by all the world for being thus troublesome, un-mannerly, and foolish. His body was of a piece with his soul, ugly and ill-fashioned ; he was as poor in respect of the blessings of this transitory world, as he was covetous to obtain them. But being descended from one of the best families in Spain, and nearly related to one of the principal ministers of state, which only helped to make him the more insolent, people showed him some little respect for the sake of his quality, although it was not recommended by the least merit. This Don Diego, who was for all the world such a spark as I have described him, thought Eugenia had every-thing a man could desire in a woman, and hoped to obtain her with ease by the credit of his friends at court, who had promised to make up the match for him. But Eugenia was not to be so easily persuaded as they imagined into an affair of that importance, and to favour a private man the court would not commit a violence that must needs have disgusted all the world. Eugenia's retiring into a convent, her resolution never to leave it, her positive orders to receive no more visits, the coldness of those that at first encouraged Don Diego in his pretensions, made him to despair of ever obtaining her without difficulty. For this reason he was resolved to carry her by main force out of her convent, an attempt the most criminal that can be undertaken in Spain, and which none but a fool like himself would ever have dreamt of. He found for his money fellows that were as great fools as himself, and gave orders to have fresh horses left upon the road down to the sea-side, where a vessel lay

ready for him ; in short, he forced the convent, carried off
Eugenia, and that unfortunate lady had become the prey
of the most dishonourable wretch alive, if Heaven had not
raised up an unexpected champion for her relief, even then
when she thought herself most abandoned by it.   One single
gentleman, whom Eugenia's cries drew after her ravishers,
opposed their whole body, and hindered them from passing
farther, with so much valour, that he immediately wounded
Don Diego and several of his accomplices, and gave time
to the townsmen, who had taken the alarm, and to the civil
magistrate to come down upon them with such numbers that quickly forced Don Diego and his companions
to surrender, or else to run the hazard of losing their lives
on the spot.

Thus Eugenia was delivered, but before she would suffer
herself to be carried to her convent, she desired to know
what was become of that valiant gentleman who had so
gallantly exposed his life for her sake.   They found him
wounded in several parts of his body, and he had almost
lost all his blood as well as his senses.   Eugenia had a
mind to see him, and no sooner cast her eyes upon him,
but she knew him to be Don Garcias.   If her surprise was
great, her compassion was no less, and she gave such tender
proofs of it, that the standers by might have interpreted it
to her disadvantage, if she had not had a just occasion
besides to afflict herself.   She prevailed with them, through
her entreaties and prayers, not to carry her generous
defender to prison, whom Don Diego, who was upon the
point of expiring, and his accomplices confessed not to
belong to their company, but to be the man that had
attacked them.   So he was carried to the next house,
which happened to be that where Don Sancho lived
formerly, and now belonged to Eugenia, who had left all
her furniture, and a few servants in it.   He was put into
the hands of the chirurgeons belonging to the court and
city.   Eugenia retired to her convent, but was forced the

next day to leave it, and return to her own house, because a new order was issued out, which prohibited all convents of nuns to receive any seculars among them. Next morning Don Diego died, and his relations had interest enough to hinder his process being made after his death ; but his accomplices escaped not so, for they were all punished according to their deserts. In the meantime Eugenia was almost distracted to see Don Garcias out of hopes of a cure. She implored the assistance of Heaven, and offered to give the chirurgeons whatever they could demand ; but their art was exhausted, and they had no hopes but in Heaven, and the youth of the sick party. Eugenia would not stir from his bedside, and attended him night and day so carefully, that she was in danger of bringing herself into the same condition ; I mean, of wanting another to do the same offices for herself. She heard him often pronounce her name in the delirious fits of his fever, and among a thousand incoherent things, which his disturbed imagination made him to say, she heard him often talk of love, and discourse like a man that is a fighting or quarrelling.

At last, nature, assisted by so many remedies, surmounted the obstinacy of his illness ; his fever abated, his wounds began to close up, and the chirurgeons assured Eugenia there was now no danger, provided no unexpected accidents befell him. She gave them handsome presents for their pains, and ordered prayers to be put up in all the churches of Valladolid for her champion's recovery. It was at this time Don Garcias was informed by Eugenia that she was the woman whom he had saved, and that she came to be informed by him how he happened to come so seasonably to her relief as he was returning home from a friend's house. She could not forbear to let him know how many obligations she had to him, and he on his part could not conceal his excessive joy for having served her so opportunely, but yet durst not presume to acquaint her with a thing of greater importance. One day as she was all alone with

him, and had conjured him not to let her be any longer
ungrateful to him, but to make use of her upon some important occasion, he thought it a proper time for him to
discover the real sentiments of his soul. He sighed at the
very thought of what he was going to do, he looked pale,
and the disorder of his mind was so visible in his countenance, that Eugenia was afraid something extraordinary
ailed him.   She asked him how his wounds fared ?

"Alas, madam," answered he, "my wounds are far from
being my greatest misfortune."

"And what is the matter?" said she to him, very much
affrighted.

"It is a misfortune," replied he, "that is without remedy."

"It is true," answered Eugenia, "you were unfortunate
to be so dangerously wounded for an unknown person,
who was not worth your exposing your life for her ! But
still, it is a misfortune that can't last always, for your
chirurgeons don't doubt but that you'll be well in a little
time."

"And this it is that I complain of," cries Don Garcias :
"if I had lost my life in serving you," continues he, "I had
died gloriously, whereas I must drag on a wretched life
against my will, and live to be the most unhappy man in
the world."

"With all the good qualities you possess, I cannot believe
you to be so unhappy as you talk," replies Eugenia.

"How, madam," says he to her, "don't you think that
man very unhappy who knows your value, who esteems
you more than any one living, who loves you better than
his life, and with all this who cannot pretend to merit you,
though Fortune had been as favourable as she has hitherto
been averse to him ?"

"You mightily surprise me," said she to him, blushing,
"but the great obligations I have to you give you a privilege
over me which under my present circumstances I should
allow in none but yourself. Only think of getting well,"

continued she, " and rest assured your misfortunes shall not trouble you long, when it is in Eugenia's power to put an end to them."

She would not stay for his answer, and by that means saved him a world of compliments ; which fell out luckily for him, because he must have strained hard to make good ones, and that perhaps might have done him harm in this present weakness. She called to some of her servants to look after him, and went out of the room just as the chirurgeons came in. Satisfaction of mind is a sovereign remedy to a sick body. Don Garcias gathered such hopes of the happy success of his amour from Eugenia's words, that from the deep melancholy wherein he had been plunged before, like a despairing lover, he now gave up himself to joy, and this joy contributed more to his cure than all the remedies the chirurgeons could use. In a little time he was perfectly cured, and out of mere good manners quitted Eugenia's house, but not his pretensions to her heart. She had promised to love him, provided he did not make any public discovery of it ; and after all perhaps she loved him as much as he could love her ; but having lately lost her husband, and been engaged in some adventures which rendered her the common subject of con-versation in court and city, she thought it not advisable to expose herself afresh to the malicious censures of the world, by a marriage so unseasonable, and against the rules of decency.

At last, Don Garcias overcame all these difficulties by his merit and constancy. He was so well made in his person as to make any rival whatever despair. He was a younger brother of one of the best families of Arragon, and although he had not actually signalized himself in the wars, yet the long services his father had done the crown of Spain might very well make him hope to find a reward of as great profit as honour at court. Eugenia could not defend herself against so many noble qualities, nor was she willing to be any longer in his debt after she had received so many obligations from him. In short, she married him. Both court and city approved her choice ; and that she might not have any reason to repent it, not long after the King of Spain bestowed a commandery of St. Jago upon Don Garcias. And before that happened, it so happened that our bridegroom convinced Eugenia the first night of his bedding her, that he was another sort of a man than Don Sancho, and she found in him what she had not found in the Portuguese Andrada. They had abundance of children, because they took abundance of pains to get them ; and the people of Spain to this day tell their history, which I have given you here, for a true one, as it was given me.

NOVEL V.

THE GENEROUS LOVER;

OR,

THE MAN OF DEEDS, AND NOT OF WORDS.

UNDER a King of Naples, whose name I cannot tell, however suppose it might be Alphonso, Leonard de St. Severin, Prince of Tarento, was one of the greatest lords of his kingdom, and one of the celebrated generals of his time. He died, and left the principality of Tarento to his daughter Matilda, a young princess about seventeen years old, as beautiful as an angel, and as good-tempered as she was beautiful. She was so extremely good conditioned, that those that did not know she had an infinite deal of wit would not have been apt to have called her having any in question. Her father, long before his death, had promised her in marriage to Prosper, Prince of Salerno. He was a person of a haughty, disagreeable temper, and the sweet and gentle Matilda, by virtue of her being long accustomed to bear with him, was so well prepared to love and fear him, that never did slave depend more upon the imperious will of his master, than this young princess did upon that of old Prosper. I think a man of the age of forty-five may very well be called old, especially where he is mentioned

with one so young as Matilda. Her affection to this
superannuated lover may be said to have proceeded rather
from custom than inclination, and was as sincere as his was
interested. Not but that he was as fond of her, too, as it was
possible for him to be, and this was no more than what any
man would have been, as well as he, for indeed she was all
over amiable ; but it was not in the nature of the beast (I
beg his pardon for this expression, but it is out) to love very
much, and he rather esteemed a mistress for her dirty acres
and unrighteous mammon, than for her merit and beauty.
The truth is, he made love but awkwardly ; Matilda however
was so happy, or, to express myself more properly, she was
so easy to be pleased, that although he did not pay her half
the respect and complaisance which one might expect from
a generous lover, yet for all that he was absolute master of
her heart, and had brought her to such a pass as to submit
to all his ill conditions. He found fault with all her actions,
and plagued her incessantly with those musty advices that
old men in their great wisdom so often inculcate to the
young and which they so little care for. In short, he would
have been a greater thorn in her side, than a peevish,
malicious governess, if he could but have found any faults
in her conduct. It is true, when he was in good humour,
he would tell her stories of the old court, play on his guitar,
and dance a sarraband before her. I have already told you
his age, but to go on with his character. He was spruce in
his person and clothes ; curious in his periwigs, an infallible
sign that his hair was none of the best ; took mighty care
of his teeth, though time began to play tricks with them ;
valued himself upon his lily-white hands, and suffered the
nail of his left little finger to grow to a prodigious length,
by the same token he thought it one of the prettiest sights
in the world. He was nice to admiration in his feathers
and ribbons, punctually twisted up his moustachios every
night, was always perfumed, and ever carried some tit-bit
in his pocket to eat, and some verses to read. As for

himself, he was an execrable versifier, a walking magazine of all the new songs, played upon most instruments, performed his exercises with a grace, but his chief talent was dancing. He loved the wits that asked him nothing, had performed some actions in his time that were brave, and some that were otherwise, and, as one might say, had two buzzards for one hawk, or if you please two blanks to one benefit. In short, I may properly apply to him a burlesque song of my own making, the latter part of which is almost worn into a proverb.

SONG.

" Here lies a fine wight,
 That could sing you at sight,
 And dance like a sprite,
 Could verses indite,
 And bravely recite.
 What's more, he could fight
 (I swear by this light)
 Like fury, or knight.

" He knew what was what,
 Could gallop or trot,
 And toss off his pot,
 And swear at the shot.
 Yet with all he had got,
 It was the hard lot,
 Of this boaster, God wot,
 To be a damned sot."

With all these fine qualities, one of the loveliest princesses in the world was desperately in love with him. It is true, indeed, she was but seventeen years old ; but our noble Prince of Salerno did not stand much upon that. There is no doubt but the Princess Matilda, being so rich and beautiful as she was, would have had a hundred gallants more, if it had not been universally believed in Naples that her marriage with Prosper was as good as concluded in her father's time, or if that prince's quality had not discouraged other pretenders, who (though they wanted his title) were men of fortune and birth good enough to be his rivals. Thus the greatest part of these lovers, either governed by a principle of fear or discretion, were content to sigh for her in private, without daring to speak. Hippolito was the only man that had the courage to own himself in public the rival of Prosper, and the respective lover of Matilda. He was descended from one of the best families in Spain, and came in a direct line from the great Ruis Lopez d'Avolos, Constable of Castile, who was so remarkable an instance of the inconstancy of fortune, since, from the richest and most powerful grandee of his own country, he was turned out of it poor and miserable, forced to borrow of his friends, and fly to the King of Arragon, who took him into his protection, and gave him a fortune sufficient at Naples to support him suitable to his quality. This Hippolito was one of the most accomplished cavaliers of his time ; his valour had gained him reputation in several parts of Europe, and all the world owned him to be a man of the nicest honour.

As I have already told you, he was a humble admirer of Matilda, and though he could never hope to succeed so long as she loved Prosper, yet he resolved to love her on to the end of the chapter. He was liberal even to prodigality, whereas his rival was thrifty even to avarice. He omitted not the least opportunity to show his magnificence to Matilda, and although he carried it as far as his fortune would give him leave, yet she seldom saw it ; for her tyrant Prosper hindered her from giving any countenance to these gallantries of love, let them come from what quarter of the world they would. Our obstinate lover frequently ran at the ring before his mistress's window, often gave her serenades, and diverted her with tilts and tournaments. The cipher and colours of Matilda were to be seen in all his liveries. The praises of Matilda rang through all Italy, in the verses he composed, and in the airs and songs he caused to be made ; but she was no more moved with all this than if she had known nothing of the matter. Nay, by the express order of the Prince of Salerno, she must go out of Naples, whenever there was to be any running at the ring, dancing, or any gallantries of the like nature, which the amorous Hippolito provided for her. To make short of my story, she affected to disoblige him upon all occasions, with a cruelty that seemed to be a violence upon her nature, and made all the world to exclaim against her. This did not in the least discourage Hippolito, and the ill-treatment of Matilda increased his love instead of lessening it. He did more than this : he showed that respect to Prosper which he did not owe him ; and to please Matilda, paid him the same deference which is usually shown to persons of superior quality, although there was no other difference between the Prince of Salerno and him than in their estates. In short, he respected his mistress in his rival, and perhaps forbore to hate him because he was beloved by Matilda. But Prosper was not so complaisant. He hated Hippolito mortally, made a hundred scurvy jests upon him, nay—would never have scrupled to tell lies of him, if he had thought any one would have believed them. But Hippolito was the delight of Naples, and his reputation was so well established there, that, although he had actually deviated from his character, he could hardly have destroyed it.

Thus Prosper was the happy man, and stood possessed of Matilda's affection, though he did nothing to deserve it. That beautiful princess did not think she saw him often enough, though she saw him every day, when fortune all on the sudden threw her from the height of happiness into the extremity of misery. She had a cousin german by her father's side, who might have passed for a man of merit, had he been a person of less ambition and avarice ; he had been bred up with the king, was of the same age, and had insinuated himself so far into his good graces, that he was the sole manager of all his pleasures and sports, and the dispenser of all his favours. This Roger de St. Severin

for so he was called, was possessed with a fancy that
the principality of Tarento belonged to him, and that a
daughter could not legally inherit it to the prejudice of the
male line.   He spoke to the king about it, who encouraged
him to claim his right, and promised to support him by his
authority.   The affair was kept secret ; Roger made himself
master of Tarento, and had placed a good garrison there,
before Matilda had the least mistrust of it.   Our poor
princess, who had never been in any trouble before, was
as it were thunderstruck with this news.   No one but
Hippolito declared in her favour, who scorned to truckle to
the king's favourite ; and Prosper, who was more obliged
to her than any man living, did even less for her in
this case than any man, whereas Hippolito not only discharged his duty, but was carried by his zeal beyond it.
He waited on her to offer her his service, but she durst not
accept it, for fear of disobliging her Prince of Salerno, who
since her misfortune did not visit her so often as he had
used to do when she was peaceable mistress of Tarento.
In the meantime Hippolito talked boldly of the injustice
was done her, and sent a challenge to Roger ; for which
he had guards placed upon him, and was commanded to
desist ; but as he was generally beloved by all people, he
might have easily raised a party in Naples strong enough
to have made the favourite doubt the success of his ill
designs.   He made several attempts upon Tarento, all
which miscarried by reason of the great care Roger had
taken to prevent all accidents of that nature.

At last the breach between the two pretenders growing
wider every day, and most of the Italian princes interesting
themselves one way or the other, the Pope employed his
mediation to procure a peace, made them lay down their
arms, and prevailed with the King of Naples to refer the
decision of the dispute between his favourite and Matilda
to judges of known integrity.   The reader may easily guess
what an extraordinary expense Hippolito had been at,

being head of the party, and so liberal in his temper ; he may likewise easily imagine that Matilda, as much a princess as she was, was in a short time reduced to very pressing necessities. Roger had possessed himself of her lands. He had persuaded the king she kept private intelligence with his enemies ; her rents were no longer paid, and no one durst lend money to the woman whom the favourite had a mind to ruin. Prosper abandoned her at last, but she still loved him so violently, that she less resented his ingratitude, than forgetfulness.

Hippolito would not offer her money, because he knew she would refuse it, but went a more generous way to work. He sent her some by one of his friends, who took the honour of it upon himself, and without telling her it came from Hippolito, obliged that princess by oath never to speak of it, lest his kindness might draw upon him the indignation of the favourite.

In the meantime the process came on, and sentence was given in favour of Matilda. The king was displeased at it, Roger was enraged, the court was astonished, every one was vexed or rejoiced according to his own inclination or interest, but yet the generality of people admired and praised the probity of the judges. Matilda, who to her glory had obtained so important a process, sent a gentleman to Prosper, in a transport that can hardly be imagined, to acquaint him with the happy success of her affair. Prosper rejoiced exceedingly at the news, and to testify his satisfaction to this gentleman, hugged and embraced him after a strange rate, and moreover promised to serve him whenever an opportunity should offer. Hippolito knew nothing of the matter till after his rival, yet he bestowed a diamond ring of great value upon the person that brought him the news. He feasted all the court, prepared lists before Matilda's window, and for eight days together ran at the ring against all opposers. Gallantries of this nature generally make a great deal of noise. Several princes of

Italy, and most of Matilda's relations and friends were there present, and signalized themselves. Nay, the king himself, who passionately admired this sort of exercise, was pleased to honour it with his royal presence. Roger had interest enough with his master to have hindered him, but by a cunning fetch of politics he had reconciled himself to Matilda, and declared to all the world, that unless he had really thought Tarento had belonged to him, he would never have attempted to make himself master of it. The king was mightily pleased with his so readily submitting to the sentence of the judges, and that he might recompense him for the loss of his trial, and his pretensions upon Tarento, gave him one of the most important governments of the kingdom, besides the places he had before. Hippolito performed wonders at running at the ring, and carried away the sole honour of it. Prosper had a mind to dispute it with him, so all be-plumed and be-feathered that any one would have taken him for an American prince. But he was thrown the very first course, either through his own fault or that of his horse, and was sufficiently bruised to boot, or at least pretended to be so. He was carried to Matilda's house, who out of vexation quitted her balcony, and cursed the amorous Hippolito a hundred times for his pains. He came to hear of it, and was so concerned that he broke up the assembly, and retired in the greatest despair to a fine house he had within a league of Naples. In the meantime Prosper was so enraged at his fall, that he treated Matilda after a most terrible manner, telling her she was the cause of his disgrace, and reproached her with being in love with Hippolito. Matilda, always gentle, always humble, and always blindly fond of her haughty tyrant, begged his pardon, and, in short, was as chicken-hearted as he was brutal. Hippolito had a sister that was bred up with the Queen of Spain, and was lately returned to Naples, for reasons I do not know, but which would signify nothing to our history if I did. Besides she

was beautiful to a miracle, and was a lady of so extraordinary merit, that rendered her deserving of the vows of
the best men in the kingdom. At her return from Spain,
she found her brother's affairs in so low a condition, that
when he set up the running at the ring, she would not
appear at court, because she wanted an equipage suitable
for a person of her quality, yet always kept at her brother's
house, which was all was left him of his estate, for he had
already parted with his lands. She came *incognito* to see
the running at the ring, and observing her brother to break
up the assembly, and leave Naples so abruptly, followed
him home, and found him in the most lamentable condition
that could be. He had broke his lances, tore his feathers
and hair, mangled his clothes and face ; and, in short,
was in such a distraction, that she would have despaired
of ever seeing him come to his senses again, had she not
known very well that a smile, nay, an indifferent look
from Matilda, would have made him to forget a thousand
ill-treatments. She did all that lay in her power to bring
him to good humour, gave way to his passion instead of
combating it, railed at Matilda when he stormed against
her and said all the good things she could think of her
when after all his transports the scene changed, and she
found him the most amorous lover that ever was.

But the surly Prosper had not the same complaisance
for Matilda ; his fall still broiled in his stomach, and he
daily laid it to her charge, though she was by no means
accessary to it. One day, when after having thanked her
judges, she went to wait upon the king to thank him likewise, although he had been against her—but at court it is
a point of indiscretion to speak one's real thoughts, or receive a denial otherwise than with fawning and cringing—
one day, therefore, when she was in the king's ante-chamber,
she saw the obsequious Prosper come in. Ever since his
fall he had never made her a visit but to scold and quarrel
with her for suffering Hippolito to run at the ring under

her window. Nothing could be more unjust than Prosper's complaints. It was not in Matilda's power to hinder a public diversion, even though it had not been designed for her sake, since her palace took up one side of the great square. And although it had been in her power, yet ought she not to have done it, unless she had resolved to be thought a woman of neither manners nor gratitude. Prosper was the only man who by his false way of reasoning fancied she had done him an irreparable injury, and his anger soured him to that degree that he went no more to visit her, as if he had broke with her for good and all. The poor princess was ready to run distracted about it, and no sooner saw this tyrant of hearts, who was just going into the king's chamber, but she threw herself in his way and stopped him. He endeavoured to avoid her, and pressed forward. She caught him by the arm, and casting a look at him that was enough to have charmed any one but this haughty brute, asked him what she had done, that he should shun her thus.

" What have you not done?" replied this prince arrogantly ; " and how can you ever retrieve the reputation you have lost by suffering the gallantries of Hippolito ? "

" I cannot hinder them, nor prevent his loving me," answers Matilda, " but it is in my power not to approve either his love or gallantry ; and I think," continues she, " I sufficiently testified my dislike of them, when I went from my balcony before the show was over."

" You should not have appeared there at all," replies Prosper ; " and the reason why you went away at last was only because you saw all the company pointed at you for being there. But your love for Hippolito has made you to lose all your reason, and his gallantries have quite effaced the services I am capable of doing you."

Matilda was vexed to the heart to hear this, and was going to answer, but he would not give her leave Besides the anger that appeared in his countenance made the princess so afraid of him that she was perfectly speechless. "When you were no more mistress of Tarento," said he to her, " and the king ordered you to be apprehended, I had a mind to see how far your indiscretion and mean spirit would carry you, and whether adversity could cure your faults. For this reason I made no feasts like your gallant, nay I pretended to be no longer in your interests. In the meantime Hippolito made a mighty bustle, and did you little service, and your affairs for a long time seemed to be in a desperate condition. Then you could condescend to make some advances towards me, in order to bring me back to you again, but this was only a copy of your countenance, since you still preserved your Hippolito. Your politics, I confess, were not amiss. You drained this poor despicable gallant while he had a drop to part with, flattering yourself, that after you had exhausted him to all intents and purposes, you should do me an extraordinary favour to take me in his room ; and you made account, that although you should lose Tarento at your trial, yet your beauty would make you princess of Salerno, whenever you pleased. But no sooner did a favourable decree revive your hopes, than you changed your maxim of state for your maxim of love. You thought a young ruined prodigal would better fit your turn than me, and considered, that if you married the prince of Salerno, you must expect to live with a master, authorized by custom, and the laws, whereas you would find in Hippolito a supple slave that would make it all his business to please you. Imprudent princess !" continued he, " durst such a poor needy wretch as Hippolito pretend to make love to a woman of your quality unless you gave him encouragement, and can any one believe, that for bare hopes only, he would have put himself to such an expense, that he is utterly beggared by it, and so foolishly too, that he enriched, with one single present, the man that came from you, to bring him the news that you had gained your cause ? Yet after all these testimonies I have of your indiscretion and infidelity, you are vain enough to believe I love you never the worse for them. Be happy if you can with your Hippolito, but delude yourself no longer that I will be unhappy with Matilda."

He would have left her after he had spoke these words, but the princess still kept her hold, and once in her life had the courage to contradict him.

"Ungrateful prince!" said she to him, 'one of the greatest proofs I can give thee that I yet love thee, is not to hate thee, after thou hast said so many disobliging things to me. They rather make against thee than me, and I cannot employ them better to thy confusion and my own advantage, than by confessing they are true. Yes," continued she, "Hippolito has loved me ; Hippolito to serve me, neither feared the hatred of a favourite, nor the indignation of a king ; he respects me, he does everything to please me. He would have protected me when I was abandoned by all the world, nay, he has done more, for he has ruined himself for my sake. What didst thou ever do like this ? Thou wilt tell me perhaps thou lovest me ; how ! Love me, and not show common civility to me ; thou who oughtest to have shown it to my sex, although it were not due to my quality. And yet what ill-conditioned master ever treated slave more unworthily than thou hast done me, and who would have thus trampled on a person that loves thee so well as I do ? No, no, prince, thou hast no reason to complain, and art obliged to me that I don't. But I will go farther than this : I will own, if thou wilt have me, crimes I never committed. I will never see Hippolito more, nay will be ungrateful to him, that thou mayest not be so to me. In fine, to regain thy heart, there is nothing so difficult but I will put it in execution."

"And there is nothing impossible to those bright eyes," says the prince to her, adjusting his periwig. "They have already disarmed me of my anger, and provided they always keep their favourable glances, the too happy Prosper will never adore any other than the beautiful Matilda."

The amorous princess thought herself over-paid with these few compliments of her old gallant. In a less public place perhaps she would have thrown herself at his feet, to thank him for this mighty condescension, but neither time nor place would give her leave to answer here. The king came out of his chamber. She begged Prosper to stand by while she spoke to him, but he shrinking away told her, it was not convenient for them to be seen together, for some reasons he could tell her. She perceived well enough, he was afraid of making his court ill, but she was so near the king, that she had not time to reproach Prosper with being a better courtier than a lover.

She presented herself to the king, paid her respects to him, and made her compliment of thanks. The king received her very coldly, and his answer was so ambiguous, that it might as well be interpreted to her disadvantage as otherwise. But the sweet things Prosper had said to her, gave her such satisfaction, that his last ingratitude, in refusing to introduce her to the king, made no impression upon her, no more than the ill reception his majesty had given her, so much transported was she to be reconciled to her imperious lover. That day she was visited by all the ladies of quality in Naples, who agreed to go a-hunting next morning a-horseback, in a campaign dress, and caps set off with feathers. The greatest gallants at court were there, so we may easily imagine, the Prince of Salerno, who was gallantry itself, made one of the company. This was not all ; he resolved to make the princess a present, which he had never done before. He sent her a most passionate letter, accompanied with a fine cap ; but to tell truth, he himself had sorted and ordered the feathers, by the same token there was not one new amongst them. As I take it, I have already observed, he had an admirable fancy in feathers. This was the only vanity on which he would lay out his money, though to do him justice, he husbanded his plumes to a miracle, for he would often diversify, and transplant them from one cap to another, and let them be never so old, knew how to make them appear fresh and gay upon occasion, as well as if he had served seven years apprenticeship to the trade. I am willing to believe he sat up the best part of the night to put this cap in order, that nothing might be wanting to so magnificent a present. The princess received it as if it had been sent her from heaven, gave him a hundred more thanks than it deserved, and promised in a letter she sent in answer to his, that she would honour herself with this miraculous cap as long as she lived. I will not tell you what sport they had in the chase, because the particulars never came to my knowledge. But we may reasonably suppose some of their horses foundered, that the cavaliers were so well-bred as to wait upon the ladies, that Prosper displayed all his gallantry, and that he engrossed the whole discourse to himself, being the greatest talker of his age.

Our ladies were so well pleased with the sport, that they resolved to take their pleasure the next day; and in order to change their diversion, designed to go by sea to Pozzuolo, where the princess Matilda promised to give them a collation and music. They no less spruced themselves up for this voyage, than they had done the day before for hunting. The boats they went in were finely adorned, covered with rich tapestry, whether of Turkey or China, I won't be positive, and the meanest cushions were of silk or velvet. Prosper would needs go thither by land, and had none but his dear self to accompany him, either to save money, or because he was melancholy, for some folks are so out of pride. He was mounted upon his finest horse, had dressed himself in his richest campaign suit, and loaded his head with the spoils of many an ostrich.

Hippolito's house lay on the road to Pozzuolo, near the sea, and the prince of Salerno must of necessity ride just by it. He no sooner saw it, but a noble thought came into his head. He knew Hippolito was at home, and therefore alighted from his horse to have a little conversation with him. Hippolito received him with all the respect and civility due to his quality, although the other had not the manners to return it. Prosper made him a very rude compliment upon his presuming to be in love with a princess, who was to be his wife. Hippolito bore his impertinence for a long while, and answered him with all the sweetness imaginable, that he ought not to be offended at his gallantry, which a love without hopes put him upon. But at last Prosper's insolence forced him to change his language, and he had already called for his horse to go out and fight him when word was brought, that the sea was very tempestuous, and that the boats wherein the ladies were, which they could behold from the shore, were in danger of being dashed against the rocks. Hippolito did not doubt but that these ladies were Matilda and her company ; he persuaded Prosper to run to the relief of their common mistress, but who excused himself upon his not being able to swim, and that he was not yet recovered of the bruise he had received when he ran at the ring. The generous Hippolito, detesting in his soul the ingratitude of his rival, ran or rather flew to the sea-shore. His servants followed, threw themselves into the sea after his example and by the assistance of some fishermen, who happened by good luck to be at that time upon the coast, they made a shift to save Matilda's life, and the ladies in her company. Their boats were overturned within a hundred yards of the shore ; and Naples had bewailed the loss of all its beauties at once, had it not been for this seasonable relief.

Hippolito was so happy, that Matilda owed her life to him. His love made him soon to distinguish her from the other ladies, whom the waves were going to dash against the rocks that bounded the shore. While the fishermen and his servants helped the first persons they found, he caught hold of the princess just as she rose above water and holding her with one hand, while he swam with the other towards the shore, he happily gained it without any one to help him. Matilda found herself much more ill upon her shipwreck, than the rest of the ladies that were saved with her. After they had vomited their salt-water, changed their clothes and recovered from their fright, they were well enough that very day to take coach for Naples. As for the princess of Tarento, it was a long while before they could bring her to herself. Even then they much doubted her life, and Hippolito and his sister Irene took all the care of her that was possible. He sent to Naples for the ablest physicians, besides him that belonged to the princess, and quitted his house entirely to her and some of her domestics that came to wait on her. He and his servants made shift to lodge at a little farm not far from his own house, whence he sent every moment to inquire how the princess did, when he could not go thither himself. As for Prosper, who was very well pleased with the rough compliment he had passed upon Hippolito, he left Matilda and the rest of the ladies to shift for themselves as well as they could, without troubling his head what became of them ; thinking, perhaps, that since he was none of the fittest to help them, he ought not to pollute his eyes with so sad a spectacle, and so jogged on gently towards Naples, expecting the doubtful event of the shipwreck to rejoice at, or otherwise, according as it would have made him happy or unhappy. In the meantime Matilda, assisted by her youth, and the remedies that were given her, recovered both her health and beauty at once, and was extremely satisfied with the great care of Hippolito and his sister, who dexterously insinuated to her with what indifference Prosper had beheld the peril she was in. Matilda did not discover the least token of resentment in her face or discourse ; whether it were because her love had mastered it, or because she dissembled her ill-usage, I cannot tell.

The night before she designed to leave Hippolito's house to return to Naples she could not sleep, and therefore

called for a book and a candle to divert her. Her women
were gone out of her chamber to sleep or do something
else, when she saw Prosper come into the room. We may
easily guess what a surprise she was in, to see him at so
unseasonable an hour, and how much she looked upon herself affronted by so disrespectful a visit. She spoke to him
of it with some warmth. Prosper was warmer than she,
and as if this princess had thrown herself into this danger
of losing her life on purpose to give Hippolito the glory
of saving it, reproached her with her shipwreck, as a blemish
on her honour, and taxed her with infidelity, by reason she
was in the house of one that was in love with her, lodged
in his chamber, and lay in his bed. Matilda would not
condescend to show him how unjust his reproaches were
but retorted on him for not having endeavoured to save
her, and in a cutting way of raillery, complained of his not
being able to swim, as also for not being fully recovered of
his late dangerous fall. Prosper reddened with anger and
confusion, treated her with opprobrious language, and told
her he would never see her more, since Roger, the king's
favourite, offered him his sister, and with her all the
advantages he might expect from the alliance of a person
in his post. Matilda could not hold out against so terrible
a menace ; her blood curdled within her, and her love soon
conquered her indignation. She had begun to exert herself
a little, but all on the sudden became a suppliant. He re-
lented too on his side, when he saw her humbled as much
as he thought convenient, and according to his custom
cajoled her, and said the same soft things he ought to have
done, if in all the love quarrels he had had with her, he had
never trespassed against the respect and tenderness he
owed her. He made new protestations of love to her, and
straining hard to surprise her by some topping compliments,
made very impertinent ones ; for he wished her all sorts of
adversities, to the end he might have an opportunity forsooth
of convincing her how much he was her humble servant.

" For God's sake, madam," said he to her in a passionate tone, "why are you not out of favour at court ? Oh that you were still persecuted by Roger! Oh that you were yet out of your principality of Tarento! that you might see with what zeal and ardour I would solicit the king for you! with what vigour I would espouse your cause against your enemies, and whether I should be afraid to venture my person, and all I were worth in the world, to reinstate you in what was usurped upon you."

"Come, come," says the princess, "there's no necessity I should be more unfortunate than I am, to give you the opportunity of showing your generosity ; and I would not willingly put your love to so dangerous a trial." They were engaged in this discourse when a noise of confused and dreadful voices, that cried out fire, made them to run to the windows, where they saw all the lower part of the house vomiting fire and smoke, and that at the same the flames beginning to enter the chamber by the stair-case, took from them all hopes of saving themselves that way, as Prosper was preparing to do. The princess, all in a fright, conjured him not to abandon her in so great a danger, and proposed to make use of the sheets and hangings to get out of the window. The prince, as much affrighted as she, told her they could not have time to do it ; and measuring with his eye the height of the windows, and considering which would be the best way to leap into the court, told Matilda very plainly that upon these occasions every one ought to shift for himself.

" But thou shalt not go without me," said she to him very resolutely, " and I will run no danger here which the most ungrateful and ungenerous man alive shall not partake with me." She had no sooner said these words, but she caught hold of Prosper, and her indignation at his baseness gave her so much strength, that in spite of all his striving and and struggling, he could not disengage himself from her. He swore, called her names, was brute enough to threaten to drub or kill her, I don't know whether, and had certainly been as good as his word, if at the time he was struggiing with her, as rudely and fiercely as if he had been to deal with an enemy, the generous Hippolito had not come into the room. The princess seeing him, left Prosper, and came up to Hippolito, who without giving her time to speak, covered her with a wet sheet, which he had brought on purpose, and taking her up in his arms, threw himself like a lion with his prey through the flames, which now had filled all the stair-case. He had no sooner set her down in a place of safety, but he was so generous as to do the like service for his rival. It is true, he burnt his clothes, and singed his hair and eye-brows ; but I would fain know what signifies the burning one's clothes, or singing one's hair, to a man whose heart had been already burnt to a coal by love ?

While Matilda recovered her spirits, and Prosper got back to Naples, without so much as thanking his deliverer, Hippolito beheld his house burnt down to the ground, together with his furniture, horses, and in short, all that his former profuseness had left him. Matilda was afflicted at it, I will not say more than he was, for alas he scarce thought of it at all, but as much as if she had seen all that was dear to her in the world destroyed. She looked upon herself to be the occasion of this misfortune to him, and indeed was not mistaken. Her cousin Roger, who had reconciled himself to her with no other intent than to accomplish her ruin more easily, had bribed some of Hippolito's servants, that were villains enough to take his money, to lay a great deal of combustible stuff in the vaults and cellars which they were to set on fire in the dead of the night, when all the family were asleep. This unjust favourite made no conscience to ruin a poor gentleman, nay, procure his death too, provided he could but do the same to a relation, whose estate he hoped by this means to inherit ; and as if her death would not satisfy him, which had most infallibly

happened, in case his design had succeeded, he likewise
endeavoured to make her memory odious. At the time
when Hippolito's house was on fire, Roger had managed
his cards so dexterously, that messengers were ordered to
search Matilda's palace, who opening her closet found
some forged letters there, which seemed to be written to the
Duke of Anjou, and which plainly convicted her of keeping
a private intelligence with that dangerous enemy of the
government.

Our unfortunate princess received this unlucky news just
as she was going to send to Naples for her coaches to bring
her home. She was extremely troubled at it, and without
staying any longer, ran to Naples with all her servants
a-foot in the most lamentable condition that can be
imagined. Hippolito offered to accompany her, but she
positively forbade him, fearing, I suppose, to disoblige her
musty spark Prosper ; and thus our unhappy lover saw her
depart, and was infinitely more concerned at this last
misfortune which had befallen the princess, and at her
commanding him to leave her, than at the burning of his
house. Matilda no sooner came to Naples, but she was
taken into custody. She demanded to have audience of
the king, but it was refused her. She sent to speak with
Prosper, but the old gentleman pretended to be wondrous
sick, and thus Matilda beheld herself all at once abandoned
by her friends, as if she had been infected with the plague.
The very same day she received an order from the king to
leave Naples. Her own domestics basely and scandalously
deserted her ; her creditors, without any respect to her
quality, persecuted her most unmercifully : In short she was
reduced to so wretched a condition, that she could not procure either coach or horse, to carry her to a certain prince
of Italy, who was the nearest relation she had in the world
next to Roger, and who had always espoused her quarrel
against that haughty favourite.

Being thus forsaken by all her friends, destitute even of

the necessaries of life, and incapable of obeying so rigorous an order, she took sanctuary in a convent, where they would not receive her without his majesty's permission, who granted it, on condition that she should leave it that very night. She went out of it in disguise, and so secretly, that with all the search and inquiry Hippolito could make, he could not meet the least information which way she was gone. However, he resolved to follow her just as chance directed, rather than sit still at home, and make no inquiry after her. While he was in quest of her, or at least fancied he was, she thought no more of him, and Prosper no more of her. He represented her as a state criminal, made his court very regularly to the king and his favourite. And as the generality of mankind use to alter their measures with the time, he made love to Camilla, Roger's sister, and begged of the king to help on the marriage. The king, who looked upon this as an advantageous match for his confidant's sister, whom he loved the best of any subject in his dominions, spoke about it to this favourite, who always liked that which his master liked.

This sister of Roger's was one of the most beautiful ladies of Naples, and though she shared in her brother's good fortune, yet had she no hand in his wicked designs. As she was looked upon at court to be the best match in the kingdom, she in like manner looked upon Hippolito to be the completest gentleman of his time, and perhaps loved him, or at least would have loved him, if she had not observed him so passionately in love with another. She took Matilda's misfortune so to heart, and was so generous in her temper, that if she had in the least suspected it was all owing to her brother, she would most undoubtedly have reproached him for so black an action, and been one of the first that should have exclaimed against it. She was so afflicted at Hippolito's late loss, that not valuing what the world might say of her, she went to find him at his habitation that was burnt down, to offer him money, or whatever else he wanted that lay in her power to bestow on him. She met with his sister there, who little expected such a visit, much less to be invited to take up her quarters at Camilla's house. This beautiful lady could not refuse so obliging an offer, and accordingly went with her to Naples. What better course could a young person of her sex and condition take, who found herself without a farthing to relieve her, without a house to cover her, without hopes of mending her fortune, in a country too where she scarce knew any one but her brother, who was nevertheless as good as lost to her, since as soon as ever he had been informed that Matilda had left Naples, he ran in quest of her like a madman, without knowing whither she was gone.

The day on which Camilla went to find Irene at her brother's house, with design to carry her home with her, the king was pleased to honour her with a visit, and presented other our gallant prince of Salerno with all his gallantry. Camilla, who had Hippolito always in her thoughts, received Prosper's compliments with as great indifference as she expressed thankfulness to the king for condescending to visit her. The sorrowful Irene bore her company, and under all her affliction appeared so charming to the young king, that he fell in love with her. His love was violent even in its infancy. He approached her with as much respect and awe as if she had been in his condition, and he in hers. He said a thousand fine things to her upon her beauty, and this lovely young lady, who demeaned herself neither with too much haughtiness nor submission, discovered at once so much wit, prudence and modesty, that he considered her from that very moment as the only happiness that was wanting to his fortune. He stayed at Camilla's house as long as he possibly could, and the pleasure he took in conversing with Irene, was so much the more taken notice of, as the young king had always seemed insensible to love, and behaved himself with great coldness towards all the most celebrated beauties of Naples. Irene was so charming that it was impossible for a man, though never so little inclined to love, and never so incapable to judge of her merit, to avoid falling in love with her. Camilla before she knew her, intended to serve her for her brother's sake only, but no sooner came she acquainted with her, than she loved her for her own. She easily believed the king was in love with her because she desired it ; and being far from envying her good fortune, as any other handsome lady but herself would have done, she rejoiced at it exceedingly. She congratulated Irene upon so important a conquest, and had without question flattered the vanity and hopes of any lady less presuming than her. But this modest damsel could not be persuaded but that the king was more a gallant than a lover ; that he had no other design than only to divert himself, and that he would think no more of her, when he was out of her sight. But she was mistaken : for it was not long before the king came again, to acquaint her with his passion, which was so impetuous that it would not suffer him to be longer without seeing her than that very evening after he fell in love with her. He told the Prince of Salerno he was resolved to go *incognito* after the Spanish mode to make love to Irene under Camilla's balcony. Prosper was mightily pleased to be made the confidant of his master's pleasures, and to accompany him in an amorous adventure. In all probability Roger had been chosen for this affair, or at least had bore his share in it, had not he that very day taken his leave of the king to go to Tarento, whither some important business had called him.

The night came, and the king, accompanied by Prosper armed like himself after the Italian manner, that is to say, with more offensive arms than a single man can be supposed to want, came under Camilla's balcony, who had been beforehand acquainted with his coming by Prosper. She knew the method and good breeding of the court too well, not to leave the king at liberty to entertain himself with his mistress in private. For this reason she retired to another balcony, notwithstanding all entreaties Irene could use to get her to stay with her. The king reproached this young lady for her uneasiness to be alone with him, and told her, she owed at least some complaisance to a king, who had for her something above it.

"I should owe all to your majesty," replied Irene, " if I did not likewise owe something to myself, which I cannot owe to any one else."

" And what do you owe to yourself ? " says the king, " which you do not owe to my love ? "

" Why not to believe you have any for me," answers Irene.

" Alas ! " cries the king, sighing, " there is nothing so sure, and nothing I would not willingly do to hinder you from doubting it."

" If I could believe what you tell me," says she, " I should have more reason to complain of your majesty, than to thank you."

" How ! cruel damsel," answered the king, " and can a passion so sincere as mine offend you ? "

" It would be an honour to some great queen," replies Irene ; " but it would very much call in question the judgment of any one else."

" It is true indeed," says the king, " you are no queen ; but she that deserves to be one, is in a possibility of being one."

" I am not so conceited of my own merit," answers Irene, " as to expect any such alteration in my fortune, and your majesty I hope has more goodness than to divert yourself any longer at the expense of an unhappy creature."

" Beautiful Irene," says our amorous prince, " I love you as much as it is possible for the most passionate and faithful lover in the universe to love, and if my tongue has informed you what my looks and sighs could not have acquainted you with in so short a time, don't think I have any design to dispense on account of my quality with any of the pains of a long servitude, or the services and cares which the most charming woman upon earth may expect from the most respectful lover. But so violent a pain as mine wants a speedy remedy, and you ought to rest satisfied in my opinion, however scrupulous and rigid you may be towards a king, who is afraid to displease you with this declaration of his love."

He said to her abundance of things more passionate than this, which the person who overheard them might unluckily forget, as I can assure you he did. So I leave the discreet reader to imagine them ; for to make a king of Naples express himself so tenderly as ours did, and at the same time not to maim his thoughts, a man must be as much in love as he was, which I humbly presume is none of my business to be at present. Irene always answered him with her usual modesty, and without showing herself either too hard, or too easy to be persuaded, she disengaged herself so handsomely from so nice a conversation, that it increased the king's esteem for her, who parted from her infinitely more in love than he had been before. From that time there passed not a day in which he did not visit Camilla and Irene, nor a night but he came to that lady's balcony, where he employed all his amorous eloquence to persuade her of the sincerity of his passion.

One night when he had given orders to his guards not to attend him, he walked in disguise through the streets of Naples, accompanied only by the Prince of Salerno. He took so much diversion in this ramble, that the greatest part of the night was spent when he came to Camilla's balcony. He found his post already taken up by two men, or at least they stood so near it, that they must needs overhear whatever he should say to Irene. One of these parted from the other and went into Camilla's house, while his companion tarried in the street. The king stayed a while to see whether he would not go away of himself, and leave him the street free ; but finding he stirred no more than a statue, he grew impatient, and commanded Prosper to go and see what the fellow meant by staying there, and to oblige him to retire. The prince of Salerno walked toward him, with as much apprehension as if he had been sent upon some dangerous enterprise. The other seeing him come up, retired. Prosper was resolved to see who he was, the other mended his pace, and seeing Prosper did the like, very fairly betook himself to his heels, when the prince of Salerno ran after him, and coursed him into another street. In the meantime the king did not stir from his post, expecting every moment when Prosper would come back, that he might send him to Camilla and Irene, to let them know he expected them under the balcony, and in all probability was wholly taken up with his amour, for a lover does nothing else when he is alone ; when the man who had parted from him whom Prosper pursued, came out of Camilla's house, and mistaking the king for his comrade :

"Look Calixtus," said he to him, "here is your dispatch. The governor of Cajetta will order you a vessel to carry you to Marseilles."

The king, without returning any answer, received the packet of letters which he presented to him. "Calixtus," adds this unknown person, "the rest depends upon thy diligence. And thou hast in thy hands the fortune of the Duke of Anjou, thy master and mine."

"Ha ! ungrateful villain and traitor ! What wicked designs art thou carrying on against me ?" cries the king, laying his hand upon his sword.

Roger, for it proved to be him, distracted at his making so fatal a mistake, and hurried on by his despair to be more wicked than he was, thought of nothing now but losing his life, or taking away that of the king, who had loved him so tenderly. The reproaches he so justly expected for his unparalleled ingratitude and villainy affrighted him as much as the severest torments that could be inflicted on him. He put his hand to his sword almost at the same time the king did, who charged him with so much vigour and fury, that Roger, troubled with a remorse of conscience for his crime, was for a long time forced to defend himself.

At last, his rage filling him with new strength and courage, he pushed furiously at the king, whom he looked upon now to be no otherwise than his enemy ; and by the desperate thrusts he made at his sacred person, obliged him likewise to defend himself. But kings, who may be valiant as well as other men, are usually assisted by a more powerful genius than that of ordinary mortals. Roger, as brave, furious and desperate as he was, could not have maintained his ground long against his incensed prince, although the clashing of swords had now brought several persons upon the spot, who could hardly be kept from hacking to pieces an execrable villain, who durst attack the life of his sovereign. His own domestics, and those of Camilla, were the first that came with lights into the street, and were strangely surprised to see their master engaged with the king.

The unfortunate Roger no sooner saw the light which exposed him to the terrible looks of his prince, but he was utterly confounded. His rage and valour abandoned him both at once, and his sword dropped out of his hand. The king, who had the pleasure to see him wounded, after he had had occasion for all his valour to hinder himself from being wounded by him, seized him with his own hands, and gave him to the captain of his guards, who came luckily by with a party of soldiers, and had received order to watch all night the avenues leading to Camilla's house.

In the meantime Prosper ran after his man, who, flying from him as fast as his legs could carry him, unluckily fell into the hands of the watch, who were walking their rounds

that night, as their custom was, to prevent all disorders in
the streets. He seemed so astonished, and faltered so
strangely in his answers, that they had certainly stopped
him, although Prosper, who pursued with sword in hand,
and had made himself known to them, had not commanded
them in the king's name to secure him, and to be respon-
sible for his forthcoming. He immediately sent back to
acquaint the king with what he had done ; and if he was
surprised to see such a number of flambeaux in the street,
and the king surrounded by such crowds of people, he was
much more so to find what had passed between the king
and Roger ; and to see that favourite, whom all the court
so lately adored, cursed by all the company, and in the
hands of the guards, who were carrying him to prison.
That night the king did not see Irene, because he would
avoid the sight of Camilla, whom he ordered Prosper to
wait upon, and assure her from his mouth that he dis-
tinguished her from her brother, whose crime should not in
the least lessen his esteem for her. Irene writ to him in
favour of Roger ; and to oblige Camilla, did that which the
repeated instances of an amorous prince could not obtain
from her. Next day Roger was examined, and found
guilty of high treason, for maintaining a private correspondence with the Duke of Anjou, who had a great party
still in the kingdom of Naples. He had been informed by
some of them of the insatiable ambition of Roger, and
having offered him in marriage a princess of his own blood,
with certain advantages, which he could not hope from his
present master, this ungrateful favourite, violating his faith
and honour, had engaged to receive the French into Cajetta
and Castellamara, whereof he was governor. The same
judges who convicted him of treason against his prince, discovered his villainous plot against the Princess of Tarento ;
and now that mirror of constancy the Prince of Salerno,
who had abandoned her when he saw her in disgrace, to
offer his services to Camilla, whom he saw in favour, no

sooner found the king to repent of the ill treatment he had given her, and resolved not only to re-instate her in her former honour and fortune, which had been unjustly taken from her, but likewise to confer new ones upon her, than this generous lord, who had so lately importuned the king to marry him to Camilla, now humbly entreated him to dispense with his promise, and give him leave to carry on his pretensions to Matilda ; and at the same time desired his majesty, who designed to make inquiry after her, to leave the care of that to him, and give him a commission to go and find her wherever he could hear any news of her, in order to bring her again to court. The king's affection was too deeply settled on the beautiful Irene not to think of her brother Hippolito, and be concerned that nobody could tell where he was. He dispatched couriers into all parts of Italy, who had orders to inquire after him as they searched for Matilda, and in case they found him, to bring him again to Naples. He hoped by this means to convince Irene how cordially he espoused the interests of her family, and how much it afflicted him that she knew not what was become of her brother, whom she loved so dearly.

This amorous cavalier, after he had searched a long time for his princess with the utmost care and diligence without being able to find her, resigned himself to that blind guide chance and rambled wherever his horse carried him, making no longer stay in any place than his horse and that of his servants, who we may suppose were not so solicitous as he in the search of Matilda, had time to rest themselves. As for his own part, he enjoyed no more repose than a condemned criminal, and after he had passed whole days in sighing on horseback, spent whole nights in complaining to the trees and rocks of the cruelty and absence of Matilda, and in quarrelling with the inno-cent stars, that generally lighted him to bed by reason he lay in the open fields and under the canopy of heaven. One day, when he was so taken up with these melancholy thoughts that he did not consider that his servant and horses could not, like himself, feed upon so slender a diet as love, he found himself towards sun-setting near a solitary inn, which rather looked like a retreat for cut-throats and banditti, than a place to lodge travellers. Hippolito had rode beyond it, for your true lover is an indefatigable animal, when his valet informed him his horses were not able to stir a step farther, out of mere lassitude and hunger, not to speak of himself, who wanted to eat and repose as well as they; upon this our despairing lover condescended to alight, but the inn-keeper, who stood before his gate, together with his wife, and an ill-looked fellow, who seemed to be a soldier, told him rudely, he had no place to entertain him in, and that his rooms as well as stables were all taken up. Hippolito was not much concerned he could not get a lodging here, and his servant had despaired of getting one, when the soldier that stood by the inn-keeper, after he had whispered a few words in his ear, told Hippolito in Calabreze, that if he pleased he might come in, and that he should be very proud to lend his room to so fine a gentleman; and while Hippolito made scruple to accept so courteous an offer, the man of the house, that had spoke so rudely to him a little before, came and held his stirrup, while he alighted, with a smiling cut-throat look, which showed he designed to make a penny of him. Thus Hippolito was persuaded to come into the inn. He would not eat a bit, and having only drank a glass of water, for philosophers have observed that love and sorrow are very dry, he walked out to take a turn or two in a place very proper for his melancholy contemplations, which he had observed not far from the inn. In the meantime his valet sat down to supper with the landlord and his wife, and the civil Calabrian, who had so obligingly parted with his chamber to Hippolito. He fell like a man that was half starved, and did not guzzle down so much wine as he could have done, because he was

forced to call upon his master to put him in mind of going
to bed, which was a thing he frequently forgot. He went
to look for him among the rocks, where he found him feed-
ing his melancholy by reflecting on the ill condition of his
affairs and his love, and brought him back to the inn,
where they showed a vile room, with a bed yet more vile,
and which having no curtains, lay exposed to the sun and
wind on all sides.

Hippolito would not undress, but threw himself in his
clothes upon the bed, as his man did upon another, where he
slept so heartily that it would have made any man but his
master to have envied him, who for his part could not sleep
a wink: but a true lover would think he had committed an
unpardonable sin should he sleep like other mortals. In a
short time all the people in the inn were got to bed, and
everything was hushed, when some persons on horseback
disturbed their repose, and thundered at the gate like to
persons that were impatient to be let in. The man of the
house, that got up to see what the matter was, knew them
and opened the gate to them. Soon after Hippolito heard
the next chamber to his open ; several persons went into it
and some of them went out again immediately, while the
rest that stayed talked to one another. He was too much
taken up with his own private affairs to have any great
curiosity for those of other people, and had not listened to
their discourse, if one of them had not talked so loud, that
he fancied he was not unacquainted with the voice. This
made him desirous to know what they talked of, and at
last he heard them speak the following words distinctly :
" Yes, my dear Julia, I must once more say it, few persons of
my condition have been treated worse by fortune than
myself ; she has plunged me in miseries that are not to be
paralleled ; but as great and vexatious as they are, yet they
don't so much disturb me as the ingratitude wherewith the
basest of men requites my affection for him ; and this
ingratitude does not sit so heavy on me, as mine to the

man whom I ought to love. I blame myself incessantly for it, and my inquietude on this score is infinitely more afflicting than all the losses I have sustained, and all the calamities that oppress me."

The other person that took up the discourse talked so low, that Hippolito could hear nothing but a few incoherent words, that were frequently interrupted by sighs. He got up and crept to the wainscot which divided the two rooms, but the noise he made was heard by the persons whom he had a mind to listen to, so their conversation ceased, but not the sighs of the afflicted party, whose voice he imagined to resemble that of Matilda. The reader may easily guess how impatient he was to know whether he was mistaken, and to satisfy himself in so important a doubt, was preparing to go out of his chamber, when all on the sudden the door opened, and by the light of a dark lanthorn he saw four men come into his room with their swords in their hands, among whom he observed the Calabrian soldier and the master of the house. If he was surprised at so unseasonable a visit from these men, who did not seem to come with any good design, they were no less so to find him up and awake, who they hoped was in a sound sleep. Hippolito, clapping his hand to his sword, asked them what they wanted in his chamber at such an hour, and in such an equipage ; and he no sooner saw them put themselves in a posture to attack him, but he fell upon the foremost with such bravery and skill, that he soon made the room too hot for them. In the meantime his footman awaked, followed the noise, and seeing his master set upon by so many enemies, seconded him very valiantly, when, having wounded all that had attacked him, he laid the most dangerous of them at his feet. These men defended themselves like fellows that did not value their lives ; but though they had been more in number than really they were, yet could they not have resisted the valiant Hippolito, seconded by so courageous a servant. He killed another of his enemies, and the two that were left very fairly betook themselves to their heels. He was so vexed at a slight wound he had received in his arm, that he was resolved to pursue them, and in all probability had cleared the world of them, as well as he had done of the other sparks, had not these villains been so wise in their fear, as to make one leap of it down the staircase and to shut the door after them. Hippolito was a long while before he could open it, which gave the two murderers time enough to make their escapes, so that he and his man returned to the inn without them. He ran directly to the chamber where he thought he had heard Matilda's voice, but found it open and no one in it, no more than in the rest of the rooms in the house, which he searched with as much care as inquietude.

"Fulvio," said he to his man, "I heard Matilda talk, I knew her voice, and no one but such an unhappy wretch as I could have missed her when she was so near me." He afterwards repeated to Fulvio the words he heard Matilda speak, interpreted them to his advantage, as he had some reason to do, but instead of giving him consolation they only increased his affliction; for he thought this was a trick of fortune, to let him hear Matilda's voice, for no other end than to make him more concerned for not being able to see her, or know what was become of her. He looked after this princess in all the places thereabout, and was so besotted as to come back to the inn to search for her there, but not a soul was to be seen, except only in the stable, from whence Fulvio took four horses besides his own and his master's.

Hippolito quitted this inn in the most pensive condition that can be imagined. Fulvio proposed to carry off the thieves' horses as lawful prize, and represented to him that perhaps they might find Matilda, and then they should want a steed to mount her upon. Hippolito did not hear what he said, or else would not vouchsafe to make him an answer, so strangely was he taken up with his melancholy thoughts. Fulvio took his master's silence for consent, and tying the horses by the tail, drove them before him designing, I suppose, to make ready money of them the first chapman he could find. They rode part of the day together, without Hippolito's answering so much as one of the many questions Fulvio put to him, in order to divert him. They lost their way, and at last were got among a parcel of barren rocks by the sea-side, and which ended in a sandy plain.

Among these rocks, in a creek where the sea ran into the land, as they came from a narrow lane, they fell in among a company of peasants, armed with all sorts of clubs and other weapons, who at first were surprised to see two men on horseback, followed by so many horses without anybody to ride them ; but at last taking heart of grace to see so few, and themselves so many, for there were at least a hundred of them, they encompassed our adventurers in a tumultuous manner ; and holding the butt ends of their muskets up at them, some cried, "Who goes there ? " Others, " Who are you for ? " Others, " Knock them down," and lastly, some more conscientious than the rest, " Who are ye ? " Hippolito could not answer so many questions at once, and if he could these ill-bred clowns made such a confounded noise that there was no hearing of him. At last an old man of a tolerable good aspect, who afterwards discovered himself to be the commander of these formidable heroes, for then every man set up for himself, partly by speaking aloud to them, which set him a coughing like an alderman at church, and partly by the rhetoric of a good oaken cudgel, made shift to compose the mutiny. He asked Hippolito peaceably and civilly who he was, and what business he had in so solitary and so remote a place from the great road. Hippolito told him he was a cavalier of Naples, and had lost his way to Ancona. He then asked the old spark what occasion had brought so many people together, who in-

formed him that some corsairs of Barbary having landed a
great number of soldiers, they had pillaged some places
near the sea, and finding none to oppose them, and being
covetous of a greater booty, were so foolhardy as to march
higher up into the country. He added that most of those
men he saw armed had been robbed, wherefore they
resolved under his conduct to wait the coming of the
enemy, and fight them as they came back with their slaves
and the plunder of a neighbouring village, which in all
probability they were gone to attack ; that 'twas impossible
for the Moors to escape, there being no other way for them
to get back to the sea but this ; and that it was not so much
the loss of their goods that had encouraged these peasants to
attempt so bold a design, as that of their wives and children.

Hippolito offered to venture his life in their quarrel, and
they took him at his word. The old man gave him the
command-in-chief, which he accepted, to the great satisfaction and joy of our boors, who now promised themselves
mighty matters from Hippolito's military phiz. Four of
the likeliest among them, of whom the old fellow was
one, were mounted upon the four horses which the provident Fulvio had brought along with him from the inn.
Hippolito divided his men into three parties. One he
posted among the rocks, where they could not be seen by
the enemy, with orders not to stir before they came up to
them. He posted the second in a narrow passage that led
towards the sea to hinder the infidels from getting back to
their ships ; and he placed himself with his men on horseback at the head of the third, encouraging them to behave
themselves bravely, and fall in with the enemy to render
their arrows ineffectual. He had scarce given these orders,
and posted his men, but the enemy appeared to the number
of a hundred and fifty. They drove several horses before
their main body laden with booty, together with the women
and children whom they had made slaves. Being old
experienced soldiers, they were not a whit discouraged to see

Hippolito and his troop marching towards them, or else perhaps they despised so small a number. I will not trouble myself to relate the particulars of this noble battle between the Moorish corsairs and our peasants, although Hippolito did abundance of gallant actions there, which deserve to be remembered. I will only tell you that his orders were well executed, that the arrows of the Moors did them little or no harm, because they fell in with them so gallantly, that he began their overthrow with the death of their captain, and concluded it by that of their stoutest men.

Our peasants when they had been once blooded put all the Moors to the sword, whether they cried quarter or not, and notwithstanding all the endeavours Hippolito used to prevent this massacre. The dead were lamented as much as the common joy would give leave, and the wounded bound up their wounds. Hippolito received a thousand commendations, and as many thanks from these poor people, who verily believed they should not have got the better if it had not been for him. They offered him the better part of the booty they had recovered from the enemy, which nevertheless he refused, as likewise to go and make merry with them after the victory.

Just then Fulvio brought two women before him in the habit of pilgrims, one of whom had no sooner taken off a great hat which hid her face, but he knew her to be Matilda. He alighted, or, I might rather say, leapt from his horse to throw himself at the feet of this princess, who embraced him with all the marks of tenderness that savoured nothing of that disobliging treatment which the tyranny of the Prince of Salerno had obliged her formerly to offer him. This faithful lover wanted expressions to let Matilda know how glad he was to see her ; never did his eloquence leave him so in the lurch, never did he so strain to declare his thoughts, which notwithstanding he murdered. In short, he did not know what he did, so great was the disorder of his mind. He was uncertain for some time whether he

should in form Matilda of the pains he had been atto find
her, so much did his excessive modesty keep him from
valuing himself upon his services. However he gave her
at last a true recital of his adventures, ever since he had
left Naples for her sake ; and forgot not to acquaint her
what had happened to him in the inn, where, as he fancied,
he had heard her voice. Matilda gave him abundance of
thanks for these last obligations she had to him, adding
that she looked upon herself to owe both her life and
honour to him, since the defeat of the Moors was entirely
owing to his bravery and conduct. She owned that it was
she who was in the next chamber to him at the inn,
promised to inform him by what accident she had been
carried thither, and, in short, to give him her whole history,
whenever she had a convenient time and place to relate it.

The other pilgrim that accompanied Matilda was one of
her chamber-maids called Julia, being the only servant that
had fidelity enough to follow the fate of her mistress, and
bear a part in all her afflictions. 'Tis probable that Fulvio
and she were glad to see one another ; and for my part, I
am apt to believe that they said abundance of fine things
and displayed their subaltern eloquence to each other, if I
may so express myself, very plentifully upon this occasion.
Our victorious peasants that had observed with what
concern Hippolito and Matilda received one another, redoubled their courteous offers to Hippolito, who made no
difficulty to accept them for the princess's sake. Among
the rest the old man, who, as I have already taken notice,
led the peasants on to battle before Hippolito came up to
them, begged of him and Matilda that they would do him
the honour to take a sorry lodging at his house, which they
accepted. He sent one of his sons in all haste to get
things ready at home for the better reception of these
guests, and now they prepared for their journey. Matilda
and Julia were mounted upon the two best horses they
could find. Among several women, whom they had freed

from out of the hands of the Moors, Fulvio observed one whom he thought he had seen somewhere, who avoided as much as she could his looking at her, as if she knew him but had no mind to be known by him. At last he came up to her, and found her to be the inn-keeper's wife that had designed to murder them. He went to inform his master of it, and desired some peasants to look after her. Towards the dusk of the evening they arrived at the village. Matilda and Hippolito were received by our old man with all the marks of esteem and gratitude. The other peasants of the village went home to their several houses, to make merry after so notable a victory, and those that lived farther off marched homewards likewise. Hippolito commanded the inn-keeper's wife, whom Fulvio had apprehended, to be brought before him, and upon the very first threatening to deliver her into the hands of justice, she confessed that their inn was a meeting place of banditti and robbers, that her husband kept a correspondence with all the thieves of the country, and that the reason why he at first had refused to entertain Hippolito, was because he expected a famous highway-man that night, companion to the Calabrian whom he had seen at the inn, to confer with him about some robberies they had in hand. She likewise informed Hippolito that the Calabrian had a great mind to his horse and equipage, to rob him of which after he had whispered with her husband, and persuaded him to join in the action, he had lent him his room. History does not tell us what they did to this woman, after they had learnt from her all they desired to know. Hippolito and Matilda, the better to conceal their quality, made Fulvio and Julia, the old man and his whole family, to sup with them. After supper, I cannot tell whether it was a good or bad one, Matilda would not suffer Hippolito to languish any longer under his impatience to know her adventures, and therefore informed him by what accident she came to the inn, and afterwards into the hands of the Moors.

"After the King had commanded me," said she to him, "to quit Naples, and through the great interest of my enemies, I had but one night allowed me to put myself in a condition to obey so rigorous an order. I implored the assistance of some gentlemen at court, whom I thought I had obliged enough to be my friends, but I found to my disappointment, that they were only such to my fortune, and not to me. I had reason also to complain of my domestics, who had all abandoned me in this extremity but Julia. She had a brother married in Naples who had the generosity to leave his family at the entreaty of his sister, to conduct me to the place whither I designed to steer my course. He bestirred himself so effectually, that the very night I was commanded to leave Naples, I had got everything ready for my journey, before break of day. We dressed ourselves in the habit of Loretto pilgrims, by which means we were not discovered at the city gates. I walked that day as many miles as could be expected from one of my sex, who had never been used to travel before, and we jogged on peaceably after the same manner for several days together without any cross adventures to disturb us. Yesterday a little before night, we were met in a narrow way by three men on horseback, that had the looks of villains. I designed to avoid them, which I endeavoured with so much haste, and so unluckily, that my foot slipping against a piece of rising ground, I fell at the feet of one of the horses that came thundering after me. The large hat which covered my face and my head-clothes, tumbled off with the fall, and my hair fell about my shoulders. My ill stars would so have it, that these men saw something in me that did not displease them. They talked awhile together, then alighting from their horses, one of them seized Julia, another caught hold of me, while the third attacked Julia's brother, who had put himself in a posture to defend us, but whom we saw soon after fall being, it seems, run through the body. After so many misfortunes which had happened to me, and which from a happy princess, at least so in appearance, had made me the most miserable woman in the world, I had some reason to believe that all the prudence and all the precaution imaginable would signify nothing against the power of fortune; that we must e'en suffer her to act as she pleases, and persuade ourselves that her inconstancy, which makes us to feel her hatred, then when we thought ourselves most secure from it, will in like manner restore us to her friendship when we least expect it. Thus I resigned myself," continues Mathilda, "to my peculiar destiny, and when I found myself stopped and seized by these strangers, submitted without any struggling to be mounted on one of their horses because I knew they could otherwise have done it by force; and although I was in their hands, yet death could deliver me from them whenever their insolence should oblige me to have recourse to that last remedy. Julia, who fell a screaming and crying out as loud as she was able, when she saw her brother drop, yet suffered herself to be carried off after my example, though she still continued afflicted. At night we arrived at the inn where you heard my voice. Your engagement with the robbers troubled us exceedingly at first, but when we saw you had driven them out of the house, and the noise was over, Julia and I quitted our room. Finding nobody in the inn, we resolved to make our escapes out at the garden door, which then stood open, and the fear of being retaken made us to redouble our speed. We travelled all night, and part of the next day, till the heat of the sun, and our weariness together, forced us to rest ourselves among the rocks, not far from this place, where we found a convenient shade, and were taken asleep by the Moors whom you defeated."

Matilda concluded the recital of her adventures with fresh protestations to Hippolito, that she would never forget what he had done for her. However she did not tell him the name of the place to which she intended to retire, and for his part he did not ask her about it. No doubt it was to some petty prince or other of Italy, in which cattle that country abounds, for any man that has money enough may there be easily made his highness, without any other qualification to merit it. I might with as little difficulty have bestowed what name I pleased upon him, since history has been silent in the matter; but I found upon second thoughts, that his name would be no great ornament to my narration, and therefore omitted it. Hippolito offered to conduct her whither she had an inclination to go, but she would by no means suffer him; however she was forced, at the repeated instances of our officious cavalier, to take his servant Fulvio with her, and two horses for herself and Julia. I will not mortify the reader with a recital of the melancholy parting between Hippolito and Matilda. I'll e'en let her go in quiet to Ancona, where she sold part of her jewels, and bring back the poor Hippolito to the sad ruins of his house, where he arrived without a farthing in his pocket, all the earthly goods he had in this transitory world being the horse he rode on. He had scarce set foot to ground, before he met a Neapolitan gentleman who was in quest of Matilda, as well as several others, whom the king had dispatched into all parts of Italy to find her if possible. He acquainted Hippolito with Roger's disgrace, after what manner Matilda's innocence came to be discovered, the orders the king had given to find her out, and, in short, with all that had happened at Naples ever since he had left it, except his majesty's violent love to the beautiful Irene, which was nevertheless known to all the world; however our gentleman thought fit to conceal it from him, whether out of an excess of discretion, or for some other reason I don't know.

You may imagine that Hippolito, generous as he was, and loving Matilda better than his life, was extremely pleased to hear of so unexpected a revolution in her favour, although at the same time he came to know that his own condition was more desperate than ever ; this gentleman having withal assured him that the king had promised Prosper he should marry this princess as soon as ever she returned to Naples. This last news hindered the wretched Hippolito from going to court, it made his life odious to him, insomuch that he avoided all manner of company so carefully, that he was the only man in the kingdom who did not know what a great ascendant his sister had over the king.

In the meantime Matilda was nowhere to be heard of, although the gentleman that had accidentally met with Hippolito went to Ancona, whither he told him she was gone, yet could he hear no news of her, notwithstanding all the inquiries he made for that purpose. A report ran of this princess's death, and some people pretended to relate the very circumstances of it, which at last coming to Hippolito's ears, it threw him into such a fit of sickness, that had like to have cost him his life. But in short, his body at length recovered a little strength, in spite of the indisposition of his mind. He was accustomed sometimes to ride on horseback along the sea-shore, and 'twas in one of these melancholy freaks, that after he had made several reflections upon the misfortunes of his life, he resolved to go and end his days in the wars which the Grecian princes were at that time carrying on against the Turk, who now began to extend his conquests from Asia into Europe. At last Matilda was found, and Hippolito was so ravished with joy, that he bestowed his horse, the only movable he had left him in the world, upon the man that brought him the news.

The same day his servant Fulvio came to him, and was exceedingly astonished to find his master so melancholy, and in so bad an equipage, at a time when all Italy talked of nothing but the great power his sister Irene had over the king, by the love he bore her. He told Hippolito the princess's name, to whom Matilda had retired, he informed him after what manner Prosper came to compliment her from the king, how he conducted her to Naples, and, according to the laudable custom of servants, that always make haste to tell their masters ill news, he exaggerated to him the joy Matilda had conceived at the sight of Prosper, and the marks of affection she showed him. " Her passion for him is so increased," continues this indiscreet valet, " that she has newly spruced up the old cap of plumes he formerly presented her with, which he has so often upbraided her with, and which is so well known at Naples, by the many jests that have been made upon it at court. I can't imagine," says he, " where the devil she had laid it up, to find it at so critical a juncture, but to be sure she must set a mighty value upon it."

After this rate trusty Fulvio began to rail at the Princess of Tarento a little more than became him ; but Hippolito bid him to hold his tongue, and perhaps had cudgelled him, had he not given off, or altered his language. Fulvio likewise told his master that the princess desired him to come and meet her. " How ! " cries Hippolito, " and does she not sufficiently afflict me by not loving me, but to enhance my affliction she must make me see how well she loves another, and will she caress Prosper before me ? It may be so, to give him, I suppose, the pleasure of seeing me die with grief, as if their happiness wanted nothing to complete it but my death. But," continues Hippolito, " I must obey her, and see how far her injustice will go."

He was in a good vein to complain of his ill treatment, and was about to have done it, as he had just provocation, when he saw afar off a body of horse, which Fulvio assured him came with the Princess of Tarento, who, designing to see Hippolito, would needs pass by his house, in hopes to find him there. Although the king had sent his coaches for her, yet she was resolved to make her entry into Naples on horseback. Prosper looked as big upon his prancer as a holiday-hero, and being all over covered with feathers like to any Indian monarch, rode by her side. He entertained the princess with a world of treble refined compliments, and every other moment sung some amorous ditties to her, very methodically, and like a man of art. Hippolito, who was out of sorts, both as to his mind and body, would fain have declined seeing his rival, as well as appearing before so much company ; but Matilda, who knew him afar off, because perhaps she saw Fulvio with him, who had parted from her so lately, rode up to him, and Prosper and the rest of the company did the like. Matilda reproached Hippolito after the most obliging manner that could be, that being her best friend, he had not done her the honour to meet her on the road, as some of the best quality of the city and court had done. Hippolito protested he had never heard of her happy return till now, and added, that although he had known of it, he had not presumed to meet her, for fear such an unhappy wretch as he might infect and disturb the public joy. Matilda assured him he had effectually disturbed hers, if she had not been so happy as to have met him. She conjured him to come and share in her good fortune, as he had done all along in her adversity : and added, that having a design to marry, because she had found by woeful experience that a young princess, without either father or mother, had occasion for a husband of power and interest to protect her, and that having cast her eyes upon the man she designed to make Prince of Tarento, she desired him to do her the honour to assist at her wedding, which she would not celebrate without him. Prosper, as having the principal interest in this affair, joined his prayers to those of his mistress, and, contrary to his custom, spoke abundance of civil things to his rival, pretending to be overjoyed to have his good company. A despairing, unhappy man interprets everything to his disadvantage, as a sick body beyond all possibility of recovery turns the best ailments to poison. Hippolito took the civilities and obliging words of Matilda as so many cruelties she was minded to persecute him with. He could not conceive how she could have so hard a heart as to make him be the spectator of her nuptial ceremonies. He could not tell what answer to make her, and therefore looked on her with astonishment. The faithful Fulvio, who was as much scandalized as his master, cursed her heartily behind his back, and, whispering him in the ear, desired him of all love not to go ; swearing that she was a fury incarnate to ask him to see her married to Prosper. In the meantime Matilda redoubled her petition with so much importunity, that Hippolito was not able to refuse complying with her. She would have him that very minute get up upon a horse she had brought for him, though perhaps it might so happen at that time that he was not master of a pair of boots. Thus we see Hippolito mounted, very much out of humour, and out of countenance, by Matilda's side, who rode between him and Prosper. The princess still continued to talk very obligingly to him. She exaggerated the obligations she had to him, and entertained the company with a recital of all the valiant actions he had performed, both against the robbers that attacked him in the night, and against the Moors, whom he attacked in the day, although they were much superior to him in number, and with but a small body of unexperienced peasants. She was interrupted by Prosper, who with an impertinence peculiar to himself, must needs acquaint her with the miracles of that famous night, in which Roger was taken, and with what swiftness he had pursued the above-mentioned Calixtus, who was privy to the correspondence which that chief minister had kept with the enemies of the state. Matilda did not bestow much attention upon his discourse, but still addressed herself to Hippolito, although he seldom made her any answer. But Prosper, by telling the same story a hundred times over, made people to listen to him whether they would or no ; and whatever happened to be talked of, he perpetually loaded the conversation with the important service he had done the king and government, by his pursuit of Calixtus.

He had mortified the company much longer with this important exploit, if the king had not appeared, attended by all the topping persons of both sexes at court and city. Prosper, to show what a fine figure he made, rode towards the king, and then without knowing why or wherefore rode back again to Matilda, with full as little reason, and presented her to his majesty, although there was no occasion for it. She was received by him as well as she could desire or expect. He excused himself for all his ill-treatment of her, laying the blame thereof upon Roger, and told her that to make her some reparation for the injuries, which through the instigations of this treacherous favourite he had done her, he now bestowed upon her one of the best preferments in the kingdom. Matilda thanked his majesty with a great deal of humility, but much more wit. I will not here pretend to set down any of the fine compliments that her gratitude suggested to her upon this occasion. I will only tell you that they were admired, nay, and applauded by all the company, as I have been credibly informed. Prosper interposing to make acknowledgments for her, only repeated what she had said before.

In the meantime Irene rode up to Hippolito, whom she knew from behind, and seeing herself out of the king's sight, threw her arms about the neck of her dear brother, who had made her shed so many tears, and drew some from her now. Hippolito, who loved Irene as much as so amiable a sister deserved, embraced her in so tender a manner, that the sight thereof was enough to soften a heart of iron or marble, according as the reader pleases. The king, who missed Irene, and could not be long without her, looked for her in the crowd, and at length perceiving her with her brother, his amorous impatience must needs make him ride up to her. He did not receive Hippolito as a bare subject when she presented him to his majesty. Matilda, Prosper, and in short all the persons of quality about the king, observed that he talked to him after such a manner, as made some of the politicians in the company then conclude, that this cavalier would make no little figure at court. But all the king's smiles could not cure him of that mournful air which the gaiety of his rival had occasioned in him, who appeared as jolly and well satisfied as if he had the whole world at his beck. All this while the sun, who darted his rays very fiercely upon this noble company, warmed most of their heads deliciously, but especially those that were bald. All the flies from the sea-shore, the gnats from the neighbouring places, those which the horses belonging to the king's retinue had brought along with them from Naples, and those which Matilda's horses had brought with them from more distant parts ; in fine, all these buzzing insects, which we may call the parasites of the air, incommoded their faces exceedingly, tormented their horses cruelly ; and those poor tits were the most exposed that had the least tails to whisk about them. I must own indeed that the umbrellas protected them a little from the beams of the sun, but not from the burning reverberation of the earth, or from the clouds of dust, with which the *sistole* and *diastole* of the lungs commonly called respiration, filled the throats of all the company, his majesty not excepted. In a word, the place was not tenable ; but to the great consolation of those who suffered most by the sun and flies, the king, who was never weary where Irene was, had not as yet told Matilda all that he had a mind to tell her ; and therefore talking loud enough to be heard by those that were about him, he pronounced the following numerical individual speech to her, for it was faithfully repeated to me word for word.

"Beautiful princess, after the persecutions you have

suffered from me, and in some measure by my orders, and after all the losses you have sustained, you would have little reason to be satisfied with me, and I should have as little to be satisfied with myself, if I did not do all that lay in my power to contribute as much to your happiness, as hitherto I have done to your misfortunes. It is not enough that I have declared you innocent, that I have restored to you all that was taken from you ; nay, that I have increased your fortune by my favours, for if I don't see you married to the Prince of Salerno, I do nothing. By making you this present of the prince, I acquit myself in part of what I owe you ; and by rewarding him with so beautiful a lady, I think I have sufficiently requited him for all the great services he has done the state."

" Ah ! sir," said Mathilda, " let your majesty take care that while you intend to be just to me, you be not so to Prosper. Acknowledgment has its excess, as well as ingratitude. You will not give Prosper all he deserves in giving him only me, and in giving me the great Prince of Salerno, you will give me more than I deserve. I am as well satisfied with your majesty, as it is possible for me to be ; and these last testimonies of your goodness, which I owe to my misfortunes, render them so dear to me, that they will be the most agreeable things I can think of as long as I live. But, sir," continued she, "since your majesty is so religious as to pay what you think you owe, and since a subject ought to govern herself by the good example of her prince, will not your majesty give me leave, now you have put me in a capacity to pay my debts, to do it immediately upon the spot, and pay others in the same coin they have paid me ? Draw near therefore, brave Hippolito," said she to this cavalier, turning towards him, " come and thank my gratitude, after you have had so much reason to complain of my unkindness. I owe you a love of many years, which is not in the least lessened by my ill-treatment of you. I owe you, besides the expenses wherein this constant passion has

engaged you, and besides the greatest part of your estate
which you have spent to support my quarrel, and your fine
house, which was burnt all along of me ; I owe you, I say,
my honour and my life, that were both in danger between
the robbers and the Moors ; and I owe you likewise a life
which you hazarded in my deliverance. I will now take care
to acquit myself, generous Hippolito, of all these obligations ;
but those I have to Prosper, being of the oldest date, are
consequently the more pressing, and must be first
discharged." Hippolito looked as pale as death at these
last words of Matilda, and immediately reddened after he
had looked pale. Prosper smiled upon him, and gazed at
Matilda with a very amorous look, who spoke to him as
follows :

"Prince of Salerno, you would make me believe that you
loved me from my infancy, and indeed you have always
treated me like an infant. You made yourself to be feared
by her whom you called your pretty mistress ; you have
always amused her with fine compliments and songs, or
treated her with reproaches and reprimands, at the time
when she expected the most important services from you.
In fine, the greatest token of love you ever gave me, was a
present of some of your old feathers, which I promised to
keep for your sake, and have been as good as my word."
With this she took the cap off her head, which Prosper had
given her in the days of yore, and presenting it to him, "At
the same time," continued she, "that I discharge my debt,
by returning you the fair words and feathers you gave me,
I bestow myself upon Hippolito and make him Prince of
Tarento, to acquit my obligations towards the most generous
of all men, whom I have always found to be a man of deeds
and not of words."

When she had said these words, she gave Prosper his
fatal cap with one hand, and with the other took that of the
despairing Hippolito, who from that happy moment ceased
to be so, and no more dreamed of this unexpected happiness

than Prosper did of being repaid with his cap. The king, as well as his courtiers, was not a little surprised at this sudden change of the scene; but Irene's great interest with him, and the justice as well as generosity of Matilda's action, made him to approve it. Besides the commendations he bestowed upon the princess at the same time kept the Prince of Salerno in his duty, who, blushing with shame and confusion, could not tell how to behave himself, and we may suppose, had it not been for the fear he lay under of displeasing his master, he would have quarrelled with Matilda, according to his ancient custom, in case the interest of his fortune had not been too prevalent for his natural arrogance. The king took pity on him, and presenting Camilla to him after he had talked a while in private with her and Irene, told Prosper that so beautiful a lady with all her own charms, and her brother Roger's estate, might very well comfort him for the loss of Matilda. In the meantime all the court strove who should be most forward to congratulate this princess upon her just choice of Hippolito, and to assure this happy lover how overjoyed they were at his good fortune. They were most plaguily embarrassed on both sides to find out compliments to answer every one, and were forced to repeat the same thing over and over again. But the king came very luckily to deliver them out of this trouble.

"Beautiful princess," says he to Matilda, "you have taught me that we ought to discharge our debts when we are able. I therefore acquit myself of the debt I owe to Irene's beauty and wit, and this day make her queen of Naples."

This unexpected declaration of his majesty surprised, as we may imagine, the company infinitely more than that of Matilda had done. Irene throwing herself at his feet, testified to him by her respect and silence, her humility and resignation. The king raised her up, kissing her hand, and from that very moment treated her as he would have done the greatest queen in the world. All these strange adventures so took up people's thoughts, that those that were most incommoded by the heat complained no longer of it. In short, they turned back towards Naples, where all sorts of rejoicings began, till all things were prepared for the king's marriage, who caused that of Hippolito and Matilda, as likewise that of Prosper and Camilla, to be deferred, to the end that the same day might be signalized by three such illustrious weddings. The king never repented of choosing Irene for his wife. Matilda, who was of so loving a temper, that she loved Prosper more than he deserved, for no other reason than because he happened to be loved by her first, yet loved Hippolito exceedingly, who for his part loved her as much when a husband, as he had done when a gallant. Only Camilla lived unhappily with Prosper. She durst not refuse him for fear of offending the king, who had punished Roger only with banishment; and thus to save her brother's life, she rendered her own uneasy, being married to a covetous, impertinent, jealous prince, who, while he lived, was the scorn and laughter of the court of Naples.

THE END.

DATE DUE
